Ticket to Prague

Ticket to Prague

JAMES WATSON

CollinsEducational

An imprint of HarperCollins*Publishers*

First published in Great Britain 1993
by Victor Gollancz
A Cassell imprint
Villiers House, 41/47 Strand, London WC2N 3JE

Published in Cascades in 1996 by
Collins Educational

A catalogue record for this book is
available from the British Library

ISBN 0 575 05646 0

Photoset in Great Britain by
Rowland Phototypesetting Ltd, Bury St Edmunds, Suffolk
and printed by Martins the Printers Ltd,
Berwick upon Tweed

. . . a faraway country of which we know nothing.

NEVILLE CHAMBERLAIN

Speech by the British Prime Minister prior to one of the most shameful episodes in 20th century politics—the signing of the *Munich Diktat* (30th September 1939). Chamberlain and the French Premier, Deladier, without consulting the Czechoslovaks, agreed to the demands of Hitler and Mussolini for the dismemberment of Czechoslovakia. On 15th October 1939 German troops occupied the Czech Sudetenland. Nazi tyranny swiftly spread to the remainder of Czechoslovakia.

Someone is missing here.
Could it be me?

MICHAL ČERNÍK
Identification

Where do you come from?
From Prague.
Well, you ought to be brighter . . .

JAROSLAV HAŠEK
The Good Soldier Šveyk

. . . it's often safer to be in chains than to be free.

FRANZ KAFKA
The Trial

In tribute to Frances Meacham
and in memory of Ivan Blatny (1919–1990)

Chapter One

The night before she was to appear in court Amy Douglas read something which disagreed with her. She shot up, wide awake, at three o'clock in the morning. The blanket was soaked with sweat. She checked her arms, her face, her legs.

"Thank God!" Nothing had changed. "I'm still a human."

She had just happened on this book. It bore a one-word title. A long word. Amy had a soft spot for long words. She had begun to read and ever since then she had wondered whether it was wise to go to sleep.

Gregor—poor Gregor. What had he done to deserve it? The opening words would haunt Amy. Of course Mrs Ambler, her English-cum-History teacher, would have cautioned, "You shouldn't read Franz Kafka before going to bed."

But the words: *As Gregor Samsa awoke one morning from uneasy dreams he found himself transformed in his bed into a gigantic insect.*

Amy went to the bathroom, switched on the light and stared in the mirror. Same old face. Same old spots. Same long nose. "But I've got intelligent eyes, says Spen. Especially the left one!"

She had a strong desire to ask her auntie, "If you came into my room one morning and I'd turned into an insect, a horrible bug, a beetle, or a cockroach—what would you do?"

Auntie was in a constant bad mood with Amy these days. Stamp on me, wouldn't you? thought Amy. She stopped on the way out of the bathroom. Auntie was in the sitting room. Maybe she'd been reading Kafka too and had had a nightmare; dreamt of turning into an old beetle herself.

She was pacing the floor and talking to an imaginary Amy. Probably a rehearsal for tomorrow's inevitable set-to. "And I am not having your friend around here any more. Oh yes, it is *your* room, but it is *my* house. And now after what has happened. After the trouble. Two people in hospital. The police. I am too old. I am not well . . ."

He's *Black*, Auntie, thought Amy, that's all you've got against him.

"Amy, there is no place for you here any more. My stroke, you see. The doctor . . . rest. Must rest. Can't sleep. A negro in your bedroom. No! Not in my house."

Amy sits on her bed, surveys her room. My room. I've woken up and I'm an insect. Poor Gregor. Poor Amy! There is another sentence from the Kafka story which enters her mind at this moment: *I'm in great difficulties*, poor Gregor had said, *but I'll get out of them again*.

Trouble is, he didn't. Would Amy?

"Bring the accused forward, Officer!" The magistrate opens a file which lies in front of him. "Ah, Amy Douglas."

She won't admit it, but she is trembling. She tells herself, remember Gregor Samsa; at least all these people recognize you as human.

The chairman of the magistrates says, "We have given your case the most sympathetic attention, Miss Douglas. We feel that you are basically a decent young person but that you have been weak and too easily led. Over the past twelve months you have shown respect neither to your teachers nor

8

to your aunt who, despite her illness, has stood by you.

"Most seriously, you have shown contempt for the law of this land.

"It says here in your Record of Achievement that you were a swimmer of great potential. Of national class. Mr Bill Daniels, your instructor, even states you could have made the Olympics. You gave it all up. With that bright future ahead of you, you opted for bad company . . . Why is that?"

"I broke free, Your Worship."

"I'm not a Worship, you will address me as Sir, young lady." The magistrate continues as if Amy had offered no explanation for her conduct, as if she were an insect. "And here you are, in the sorriest plight, awaiting the decision of this court. Before I announce your sentence, I would like to ask you—are you resolved to lead a better life?"

What's happening to my face? I can't control it.

"You are laughing at us, Miss Douglas."

"Not laughing, Sir."

"Grinning, though."

"It's all this." She scans the court. "Just for me."

"All what?"

"All this. Well, you know . . ."

"I do not know. Tell us."

Better not. When I open my mouth these days, I damage myself.

"I repeat, have you any comment to make on this deplorable episode?"

Deplorable episode: yes, a good way to describe it. Amy stares across at her friend Spen. The woman on the bench fancies him, that's for sure. Most people do. It's his smile. Mind you, the chairman of the magistrates plainly doesn't fancy him.

Didn't believe a word Spen said, either.

9

"On the day in question," the prosecuting lawyer had told the court, "the two accused visited the Lamb and Flag public house. There was an altercation with a group of youths."

Altercation—is that what they call it?

Amy thinks back. At first there'd been the usual taunting: "What's the problem, Blondie—aren't there no whites wi' bananas big enough for you?"

It's on their shirts—Rule Britannia!

"We don't want no trash in this neighbourhood."

"I'd sooner have a dog after he's been at her."

This used to be a neighbourhood, a bustling community. But then came the new shopping centre and on top of that, the recession. The local shops closed. The pubs struggle on.

There's even a bit of history: just down the road stands a ruined priory with—once upon a time—a view of the sea. Today junkies shelter under broken arches and pray for summer.

"Somebody bitten off your tongue, Blondie?"

Spen has a belt of some colour or another for karate: is this what is keeping him so cool? "We're going right through, Amy."

"Ain't you noticed, Bozo? You've reached the new Berlin Wall, whites only beyond this point."

Three up front; two circling; two reinforcements hovering to pick up the pieces.

Amy is running, anywhere; and Spen is saying, "This is crazy!" Running, he means. Gives off all the wrong signals. They will throw me about, decides Amy, but not draw blood.

Big roads lead to small ones. Small ones narrow, shrink to tracks and paths. Another pub on the right, blokes out on the pavement—it's mild for December; their pints on the wall.

Opposite, a pedestrian precinct to the estate called Unity. Nice one. Suddenly, relief. Have they jacked it in, gone for a quick one? No sign. Amy falls on Spen, Spen on Amy, bursting.

But there's no respite. Up the hill they come, all seven of them. Another straggles behind. At a guess, three of them over six feet tall, each with a souvenir chunk of fencing from nearby allotments.

"Here, Bozo, you got trouble."

Is this a statement or a question? The voice is from the white-only crowd outside the pub.

"We got trouble," admits Spen.

"That's too bad." Is this an expression of sympathy or mere curiosity? "Two against seven, right?"

Wrong. But what the hell, this isn't a maths class. "Yeah, real British."

"Never say that, mate."

"Spen, those are scaffolding poles. Let's get out!"

Spen has also armed himself with a piece of fencing.

"Wood against steel, you idiot. Let's go!"

"Oh yeah? And have 'em round my front door?"

The warriors pause, eye the field of battle to come.

Spen isn't particularly big but he can be vicious. "Whose head's first, you bastards?"

The first assault is Amy's—and on Spen. A push that saves him from the flight of a scaffolding pole. It makes a hole where he had been standing, scuffing up the tarmac path.

"Me!" Amy is left with wood as Spen grabs steel. "Thanks." Spen does not wait. He too paid attention to Kate Ambler on historic battles: "the best form of defence is attack."

Spen is past Amy, forward of her. Into the midst of the boldest three; and he is hacking; not threatening, but doing. And they are hacking back, though one is on the ground and bleeding.

11

Amy feels the wood. Its nails, she notices, are bent. Won't damage skulls quite as much. Go for limbs anyway. Spen is surrounded. Amy hits and hits. Backside, shoulder. Avoid the head.

They are not avoiding Spen's head. He staggers but this helps him miss a fiercer blow.

"Not cricket, mateys." Can't believe it: reinforcement from the onlookers at the pub; and white. "One at a time, bozos!"

Where do all these small-arms come from?—a broken chair; a spade handle; a dustbin lid. The sky is full of things. Spen is mad. It's in him, the fight, and Amy is shouting "Leave it, leave it there, oh my God, Spen—Spen!"

Wars, Kate Ambler believes, are easy to start but horribly difficult to stop.

The word 'truce' isn't in Spen's vocabulary.

Amy is in the road, on her back, with the bent nails sticking into her and the shadows of battle flickering across her face.

But Spen's assistants are now the masters. This is cricket all right. They are beating the beef out of the opposition.

Amy screams, "Stop it!" But the world has gone deaf. "Stop it now!"

There're two on the ground, one not moving at all, except for the motion of his blood: their leader, lost for words.

Suddenly: police cars, and a van; all lights flashing.

"Spen! The fuzz!"

Didn't Kate Ambler add, "Because war's in the blood and there's no joy like triumphing over the enemy"?

Absolutely right, Mrs A: I can prove it.

And then the ambulance. The man on the floor they call Rocky. Mister Big, but he'll not be that again for a long while. The other man on the floor is Spen.

The police, thinks Amy, have this sixth sense: they know

who starts fights. Spen had been pinned to the ground. His head had been bleeding, but it bled a lot more from being law-and-ordered on the tarmac in the post-war period.

Everybody is arrested; even the cricketing mates from The Heart of Oak opposite. They're into blood, but triumphant.

Ecstatic is a better word. Five require hospital treatment and will be allowed home after repair. Rocky's more serious. His skull is fractured. Spen too has his war trophy to brag to the nurses about—a broken collar bone and a half-severed ear.

And now he has been charged with starting an affray.

Wait a minute!—*starting* the affray?

"I was there. He didn't start anything," Amy had protested.

"Sit down, please."

"He didn't start anything!"

"We will be the judges of that," snaps the magistrate, "now sit down or you will be ejected from this court."

Successfully argued by the Defence: Spen did not start the affray. Now the bad news: Spen was guilty of violent disorder, grievous bodily harm and the use of undue violence.

Two years in prison. Same as Rocky, the chief gristlehead who did start the affray.

The magistrate explained that he wished to be even-handed. At these words Amy Douglas had shot once more to her feet. She screamed loud enough to scatter the starlings bickering on the court roof:

"Piss on your justice!"

The starlings were silent, the court was aghast. The chairman of the magistrates sucked in his breath and then expelled it with a hiss: "Bring the accused forward, Officer!"

*   *   *

Amy Douglas was never to see Spen again. As for her, she was sentenced to six months' community service and a further month for using obscene language in court.

"And do you even begin to realize, Amy," asked Mrs Harvey, her headmistress, "the damage you have done to the reputation of the school with your outburst?"

"An injustice was done. I spoke out against that injustice."

"In *your* opinion, Amy Douglas. Not in the opinion of the court."

"And that is why I used the 'piss expression' as you call it . . . But don't worry, I'm leaving."

"No, you are being expelled. That information will conclude your Record of Achievement. A tragedy."

"Can I go now?"

"I have not finished. Oh, please listen, and sit down. We used to be friends, didn't we?"

"My only friend is in jail."

"He nearly killed two men, Amy—heavens!"

"Two white men who tried to kill him."

"It's nothing to do with colour."

"That's what they all say. It gives them an excuse not to do anything about the problem."

"I want to talk about you, Amy—what you're going to do now."

"I'll make out."

"I believe your auntie—"

"Has gone into a nursing home. I could have looked after her."

"Twenty-four hours a day?"

"She's looked after me twenty-four hours a day."

"And her flat?"

"It will be sold to pay for her in the home."

"Then—"

"I'll be homeless. What's new?"

"Will Spencer's mother have you? I mean—"

A big shake of the head. "Never. Spen's mother blames me."

"Blames *you*?"

"Thinks the boneheads would've ignored him if I'd not been with him."

"That's not very charitable."

"He is her darling. Never been in an ounce of trouble. Church-goer too." Laughing now. "And as you know, Mrs Harvey, he's got six GCSEs with As in English, History, Music and Art. He even wore ties!"

"Glad to see you've still got your sense of humour, Amy . . . Oh why did you smash the courtroom windows, girl? Why?"

"My sense of humour, I guess. It was so stuffy in there."

"The Governors over-ruled me, you see—"

"No need to apologize, Mrs Harvey."

"If you'd only kept up with your swimming. The team lost again, without you."

"I'll give your best regards to my auntie, shall I?"

"I'm so sorry . . . If only."

"Oh yes, Mrs Harvey: if only . . ."

Amy had been in a mood to walk out even on her favourite teacher, but she was caught by Kate Ambler at the foot of the stairs. "I never realized it was Spen you fancied, Amy."

"Maybe I should have written it in my Record of Achievement."

"Will you visit him?—because I want him to start his A-Levels. We can arrange something."

"He doesn't want visits."

"So who's going to bring *you* flowers now you're in the mire? And don't tell me you'll make out. The jungle is strictly

15

for birds and you'll find your wings've been clipped back to the shoulder."

Amy knows how to handle Kate Ambler. "Remember what Gladstone said, Miss?"

"Sure: 'My mission is to pacify Ireland'. About the dumbest comment ever made. So what quote are we to remember you by, Amy? Don't help me. How about, 'I had everything going for me and I chucked it away'?"

"On the contrary, Mrs Ambler. I'm going to do what you advise all your students to do: 'Go out and make history!'"

At last a smile. "Okay, you win. You'll make out. But do me a favour. Eat an apple a day—and learn one new word a day. That's what my grandad told me."

In class, Mrs Ambler's grandad had stood for all that was wise, a combination of Solomon, Gandhi and Mother Teresa of Calcutta. Amy, who had never had the chance to sit at the knee of an old sage beside the camp fire and listen to the wisdom of the aged, had always wanted to ask Mrs A, "What happened to your wonderful grandad?"

Now she did. In return for agreeing to learn a word a day, she got an answer: "He died of a surfeit of good advice."

"Surfeit?"

"It's Day One—go and look it up."

16

Chapter Two

"There are only two rules at High Lawns, Amy," says the bursar, Mrs Benson ("Call me Sylvia, except when the Doc's around"): "Don't believe anything the patients tell you, and don't have favourites . . . Now, because we are desperately short of staff, you'll be asked to do plenty of things you're not qualified to do and you'd be dismissed for doing if anyone was interested enough to find out.

"You'll be issuing pills and administering jabs like everybody else. Basically you'll be feeding, clothing, washing, scrubbing up what they deposit on the floor, stopping them from fighting over fag-ends and generally maintaining law and order. But with kindness, remember that.

"Sometimes, when you're dozing off at two in the morning and one of them demands to see his solicitor, his niece Marilyn Monroe or his nephew Genghis Khan, you'll experience the occasional spasm of impatience. Like wanting to bury an axe in their heads.

"Try to remember on these occasions that there's no such thing as a perfect world. As Doctor Parrish says, we are all prisoners of something or other."

Glory: peering into ribs of sunlight that waver against the blue, sky patches of it, and feeling—yes, how gloriously—

this is my element: Amy the water sprite, Amy the mermaid, Amy the dolphin.

And Amy the criminal? Ah, that's me on land.

Arms slipping down the sun, dripping diamonds. "Your element," Bill Daniels had commented. "Yet how come you aren't a Pisces?"

Slow on the turn; getting out of practice already. But the kick's there. Yes, Bill, the most powerful junior kick between Harwich and the Hook of Holland.

"You'll do that one day. Everest of the waters!"

The English Channel was more than enough, thanks. That was a bit of glory too: raised three hundred quid for charity. Orphans. Didn't know I'd become one within six months.

Fifty-three, quicken the stroke. Ninety lengths by two o'clock.

"Excuse me!"

A better turn, almost up to the old standard.

"Excuse me—young lady?"

This is a bonus. Three hours on the job and I find a swimming pool all to myself.

"Young lady!"

Stop, foot down. The sun spreads circles on the water. Amy is momentarily robed in liquid silver. "Yes?"

A middle-aged man in a brown suit is waving at her. A gaudy red and green tie clashes with his suit and his flushed face, but matches his grey hair. "Are you a member of the Swimming Club, because—"

"I'm a member of staff. Just joined."

"Oh I see. You must be the new girl. I'm Doctor John Parrish, in charge around here. People call me JP." A chuckle. "Justice of the Peace, you know . . . I'm just thinking it's a bit dangerous—swimming on your lonesome, that is. If you should sink—"

18

"I won't sink, I promise!"

For the first time Amy notices she and JP are not entirely alone together. All along the tennis court that adjoins the pool and is divided from it by a steep grass bank, are faces; hands clutching the wire netting; voices laughing and calling.

"You are proving a bit of a spectacle, my dear." Amy steps up from the water. "But don't worry. Our patients are interested in anything that's different."

"Different?"

A smile. "Well, somebody who can actually swim."

"What time is it, please?"

"Eight minutes to two."

"Then I'd better get changed. I'm back on soon."

"Miss Amy Douglas, I presume. Community Service, right?"

"Call me AD, JP."

"You're very welcome, AD. We had a BC once, a male nurse, gave swimming lessons, only he left. They all do sooner or later . . . Would you be interested—in giving our people a few lessons, I mean? We'd pay you."

"Teach them to swim?" Sylvia Benson is not so sure. "They'd wander into the deep end when you weren't looking, and drown."

"Not if I keep an eye on them."

"They'd all want to come."

"Say three at a time?"

"And if one sinks?"

"I'll fish him out."

Three days into the job and Amy's week takes a turn for the worse. "AD, a phone-call for you. They say it's Maidstone Prison."

"It must be a mistake, JP. I've done nothing."

"A courtesy call, I believe . . . By the way, thanks for offering the swimming lessons. It'll look good in our new brochure. From April Fool's Day we become a Trust establishment—private. Our masters assure us of a better class of insanity."

Alone now in JP's office. "Amy Douglas speaking."

Maidstone is Spen's jail. She is angry with him still.

"I never want you to visit me, Amy."

"That's stupid."

"Or write to me."

"What do you want to be, a martyr or something?"

"I mean it. No visits. I don't want anybody to see me in there."

"Not even your Mum?"

"I don't want *anybody* to see me."

"You'll change your tune once you're inside." Yet Spen's attitude had worried Amy profoundly. He'd said, "I'll never stand it. Not cooped up—"

"You'll get remission."

"You don't understand, do you?"

"I'm visiting whether you want me to or not. I just want you to think of me sitting out there in the waiting room, after a hell of a journey, and being told you won't see me."

"Don't waste your bus fare."

"I've no fare for any bus. I'll be hitching a lift."

Spen had kept his word. Took all day to get to Maidstone. Very sympathetic, the warders. One gave her a bar of chocolate. The only thing she'd eaten all day. "Sorry love. We've got plenty of prisoners who'd love a visit from a pretty lass like you—but no go with Spencer Rickards, I'm afraid."

And none of Amy's letters had been answered. She decided

Spen's loss of liberty was like that of the aborigines she'd read about: rob them of the open sky and they die.

The caller is an assistant to the governor. "Miss Douglas, we have your letters to Spencer Rickards and they are the only information we have as to his life outside of prison. We wonder if you could help us locate his family—who've moved home, I believe, and never been in touch."

"What has happened?"

"Oh, don't you know?" A pause. "I'm so sorry. Rickards hanged himself in his cell last night."

"JP. Would it be possible to see your way to lending me the train fare to Maidstone?"

"Your boyfriend?"

A nod. No tears. All that will come later. "He's agreed to see me at last. But only if I go tomorrow. I'd get the cash off my Auntie, only she's just settling in the rest home, and visiting's not till Sunday."

Three lies, Amy Douglas.

"It must have been rather urgent for the prison to call."

"He suffers from acute depression. He's very down at the moment and asking to see me."

"Doesn't he have a family?"

"He's an orphan."

JP produces two ten pound notes. "Very well, here's an advance for the swimming lessons."

"This way, Miss Douglas."

"He wasn't religious," protests Amy as she is ushered into the prison chapel.

"This is what most families prefer."

He looks so peaceful; and so beautiful.

"How could you let him do it?"

"There will be an enquiry, Miss."

"Amy's my name . . . Can I touch him?" She does not wait for permission. She approaches the bare pine coffin. They took away your sky, Spen. She stretches out her fingers, strangely steady, yet holds back from the cold flesh.

"He talked about you, Amy. Great swimmer, I believe."

Poor Spen. Poor Amy. All the words she can muster are, "I guess that's it then."

Amy is remembering her last exchange with Spen. "You say you won't see me, you won't read my letters. You won't write . . . Go on, make life impossible for both of us."

"I won't write letters that cops and warders will look at. Never!"

"Spen, you're like me, you're your own worst enemy."

Spen had shaken his head. "No, my skin's my worst enemy."

Amy had watched her own spit fly. "Your skin's your best feature."

The warder is indicating Spencer Rickards' sparse possessions—the clothes he wore when he entered prison and several paperback books including one given him by Kate Ambler, James Joyce's *Ulysses*. Inscribed on the flyleaf are the words, 'Prison walls *need* not a prison make.'

Thanks for trying, Mrs A.

"You want them?" the prison officer asks. There is something else—a silver propelling pencil. Amy knows it well for it once belonged to her dad.

She'd sent it to Spen and she too had attempted words of comfort: "This is your new pal. She's called Jocasta Scribblequick. Please use her to write to your old one." She had signed herself Amy Anguish, a name Spen sometimes called her when worries about the world got her down.

"What about his family?" she asks, still hesitant to take possession of Spen's things. A shrug from the prison officer, but no comment, so she scoops up the books and the silver pencil.

"I don't want him buried."

"He will be cremated, Amy. I'll have to enquire what happens to the ashes."

Why can't I cry; what's stopping me? Instead I even joke. "I think he'd want them scattered over Portman Road."

"Portman Road?"

"It's where his beloved Ipswich plays. You know, football. Preferably at the North stand end."

"I'm sorry, lass. Really."

She is Amy Anguish well and truly: "Is life all that important?"

"Burglars."

"You mean burglars did all this—smashed my auntie's place up?"

Mr Bradley, the officer from Social Security, whom Amy prefers to classify as the Man From Up There, is incapable of surprises. He is trying to be patient. "Miss Douglas, it's the world we live in. People call it freedom. I call it excess."

Evie, from the flat next door: "It was so quiet all night, I can't understand it, Mr Bradley."

"Evie's deaf."

"This will all have to be reported. According to the schedule, there are even clothes missing."

"Such as?"

Evie, quick. "Her Chinese silk nightgown—that was supposed to be for me."

Amy, snapping, "No it wasn't. It was my mother's. Auntie'd never have given it to anybody but me."

"Well she did, as she's not talking to you no more, Amy."

Evie is suspicious. We never got on. Prying old bat.

The Man From Up There is also suspicious. He thinks I did the job. "It'll have to be looked into." Mr Bradley is also in a hurry: all Auntie's things—those that have not been stolen—must be removed by ten o'clock prompt, so the new people can move in.

"What about me?"

"We've gone through that, Amy. You are not a minor any longer."

"I am homeless."

"Yes, I'm sorry. But housing is not my department."

"That's all right. They're putting me in an asylum."

Evie: "Our John says you can stay over."

Your John is a groper. I wouldn't get halfway up the stairs. "Thanks, Evie, but I'll manage."

They are looking at me. This destruction is the work of a madman; or a madwoman. It is my memorial to Spen, but I do not feel any better. "I'll get my case." I am up in my room a long time. I want to lie on my bed just once more. My posters and pictures, well they suffered from the tornado too.

It's time I got myself a new image.

"They've done my room too, you know, Mr Bradley." I think this is the only thing stopping him making a citizen's arrest. I've spared only my Freddy Mercury poster. That comes with me to hell and beyond.

I wanna break free: thanks, Freddy and farewell.

And of course my music machine which scarpered under the bed when the burglars came. There, wrap it up in the bathtowel.

"If you don't mind, Miss, I'd like to check your suitcase before you depart."

"That nightgown was worth hundreds," says Evie, seeing

her chance, eyeing Amy's bulging suitcase and bursting hold-all. "It was promised to me. It's a kimono!"

"If you don't mind, Miss," insists Mr Bradley.

Well I do mind, because I've had my bellyful this week. I've had enough. Got it? Enough of corpses and enough of these two carcass-eaters.

"Nobody—just bloody nobody—checks my private parts without a warrant." Amy Anguish becomes Amy the Assertive. I use my shoulders.

Mr Bradley is about to make a grab. "One touch, Mr Bradley, and I'll have you for child molestation. It could ruin your career."

"Words, Amy Douglas," Kate Ambler once said, "they'll either make you or ruin you."

Despite Evie's passion for the silk kimono, despite Mr Bradley's boundless suspicion, neither attempts to stop Amy. She reaches the door; pauses.

This was home. Of a sort. And of a sort is better than nothing. I tended it. Did the brasses; hoovered it. She is angry and sad. "I decorated this room. And I painted out the kitchen. Don't I get anything for that?"

As for you, Auntie, I won't forgive this. Just because you found me in bed with Spen, I am beyond mercy. *My* bed, Auntie.

Spen was gentle, which you've never been.

Amy reserves a final onslaught for Mr Bradley. "I'll be back for my books, Mister. I know every single one. And I'll take you to the Court of Human Rights if there's as much as one paperback damaged or missing. Understand?"

Mr Bradley is used to being shouted at by his clients. "The books will be in cardboard boxes on the landing, Amy."

"Thanks a lot. Maybe I'll empty one out and live in it."

Chapter Three

From a distance, High Lawns does a passable imitation of a stately home. It stands on a pleasant incline among acres of meadow and woodland, all encompassed by high stone walls. Ancient beech trees escort the main drive which stretches through rough pasture to a sunken wall. Beyond this are lovingly tended gardens, smooth-cropped lawns, a tennis court and an open-air pool.

It is eerie by moonlight; or, if you have not taken leave of your senses, romantic.

A figure has chosen not to enter through the main gates, for these are always locked at dusk and a notice at the gatehouse forbids visitors between seven in the evening and nine in the morning. Some of the walls are sprinkled with broken glass, but not all; and friendly trees grow close enough to permit intruders to leave their ladders at home.

The figure has tossed two bulky items over the wall at a carefully chosen spot—the wall-side compost heap of the aptly-named gardener Sam Peet.

A soft landing awaits a suitcase, holdall and Amy Douglas. Thanks, Sam, for not leaving a garden fork in the way. There's a smell of cabbage leaves and potato peel.

The main entrance to High Lawns is imposing: Georgian style, with a fine pillared porch. On either side of the steps are Grecian urns filled with Sam's flowers, at this time of the year a mass of blue and white aubretia.

Amy veers right through shrubbery. The ground window leading on to the stairs needs fixing and this not being the sort of place burglars wish to break into in a hurry, there is no alarm.

Something sharp and narrow shoved through the gap and—"Home!" Up the stairs, bannister of polished wood, creaking. On the second floor nothing creaks, wood having been replaced by cold concrete.

Up in the world, that's where you're going, Amy Douglas. To the top floor of a loony bin, that's where.

"Whatever you do," Sylvia Benson had advised Amy, "never call the place a loony bin. Never use such words as 'lunatic', 'mad', 'round the bend' or 'round the twist'. These unfortunates are our family. Now they're your family."

Along the corridor, where there's nothing to bump into but darkness. Sylvia had explained, "We had to have a clear-out some time ago—government policy: patients, then furniture. Those who were considered capable of fending for themselves in the outside world were required to do just that. Occasionally one or two come back and stand at the gate.

"A funny thing, freedom."

The fourth floor is where the repairs are due; have been for as long as Mrs Benson can remember: buckets in the corridor to catch the residue of heavy storms; ceilings falling in.

Amy stops at the end of a short passage, opens a door which squeaks a ghostly welcome. Pure Edgar Allan Poe. On her first exploration she had cleared away the cobwebs, swept the floor of mouse droppings and scoured the bath, the taps and the walls with disinfectant. She had rounded off with a word for Mrs Harvey, her former headmistress: "Got to have standards—agreed, Mrs H?"

"Schools these days cannot afford, I'm afraid, to lose face, Amy. And your behaviour certainly lost us face."

"I was talking about standards, Mrs H, not face. Or does that amount to the same thing these days?"

A deep breath: the smell of disinfectant lingers. "Chez moi! . . ." What do you think, Auntie? My own bath—water's still running. Sink. Loo. My very own warming cupboard. As good as a hotel.

Somebody's left a rope strung above the bath. The sight of it, long enough and strong enough to tie twice round your neck and then swing you from the ceiling, banishes Amy's frail good cheer.

You did yourself in with a tie, didn't you, Spen? I hope it wasn't the one I gave you. It was my dad's. Real silk, from Hong Kong.

She opens her suitcase: a blanket to go under; and her very own duvet. Can I risk the light? Bulb gone. She resorts to a candle. Coat hangers: always very tidy, Amy. Got it from my auntie.

First of everything—the kimono. Its deep stitchwork flashes in the candlelight. Promised to Evie?—I'll burn it first. Amy stares at her one family heirloom: black silk, with sleeves and lining of forget-me-not blue.

There are clusters of beautifully wrought lilies, white-petalled, yellow-centred and six great roses rising in shimmering contours from the valley of the robe. At the lower hem four silver-stitched junks sail on silver water.

And there's me, the salmon-pink flying fish. Like me, the water's its home.

She unzips the holdall and takes out Spen's copy of *Ulysses*. She turns to page one. Let's see, was it this that bored you to death, Spen? Our Kate never believed in light reading.

Stately, plump Buck Mulligan came from the stairhead,
bearing a bowl of lather on which a mirror and a razor lay
crossed. A yellow dressing-gown, ungirdled, was sus-
tained gently behind him by the mild morning air . . .

"And this gentleman is Josef, spelt with an 'f', one of our longest-serving customers," says Sylvia Benson on Amy's first full morning of duty.

"Customers?"

"Oh yes, that is what we have to call them these days. It sounds more business-like. Josef is foreign. He smokes too much and hates taking exercise. A lazy old scruff, really— aren't you, Josef?"

Still in pyjamas and slippers though it is past eleven, Josef makes no response to Sylvia. He is around sixty, Amy guesses. He is short, scrawny but still with a generous head of grey hair.

He spares one glance at the tall, handsome girl with blonde hair. There is the dart of a smile from watchful green eyes that seem to say, 'I know secrets but I'm not telling'.

"Josef won't give you any bother, Amy. There is little point, by the way, in trying to engage him in conversation. He's foreign and doesn't seem to have bothered to learn our language beyond 'I want', 'No' and 'Football!' He is what JP calls *homo mollusca*, someone trapped for ever in a shell of almost absolute silence."

Amy is wondering, should Sylvia be saying all this in front of Josef?

"Don't worry, he never listens to what anybody says. We call him Sir Stubborn."

Amy takes to Josef instantly: Sir Stubborn, meet Lady Stubborn.

"Shall I turn the telly on for him?"

"No, he prefers it off."

"He looks as though he is watching it."

"Oh yes. If he's watching it, or looks as though he's watching it, and it's off, don't wheel it away or he'll become quite agitated."

"And if I turn the telly on?"

"He'll walk away."

Amy grins. "That means he's got good taste. I'm not struck on telly myself."

Sylvia isn't used to considering the opinions of young people sent up on Community Service or from the Youth Training, but Amy seems different; brighter, more full of herself. "You've got a point. All that violence and suffering before your very eyes, well it's enough to make you feel suicidal . . ."

"Like you want asylum?"

"Yes, I guess that's what we are at High Lawns, a refuge from all the horror and carnage." Sylvia explains that Josef, as a special privilege, is allowed to stay up to watch the late-night football. "Otherwise he retreats into his shell completely."

Amy contemplates Josef. "He looks so intelligent."

Sylvia drops her voice. "There's absolutely nothing wrong with Sir Stubborn that a good kick up the backside wouldn't cure. Private opinion, mind."

Twenty minutes in the pool: pure bliss; the moon is up. Something about swimming in the dark. And I am in top gear because I don't want to think about things.

How's death, Spen? Is there any discrimination in heaven or haven't they noticed your black skin yet?

Breaststroke to backstroke. There's heaven—which star is you, Spen?

Drying off, ready for the overnight shift and suddenly being called by Clifford, the senior night nurse. "Day room— a punch-up!"

It is Sir Stubborn's territory on the first floor: lights on, glass smashed. Two bodies in pyjamas are struggling, right against the broken window, one trying to throw the other one out.

Clifford skids over the polished floor, grabs collars, prises the combatants apart. "Shame on you both, you silly old sods!"

Two old men, dumped in their chairs, one calm—that's Josef, the other shaking—that's Mr Dodds.

"Josef, I'm shocked. Truly shocked. A pacifist like you. A philosopher. A Buddhist dedicated to the order of silence . . . And you, Mr Dodds, what have you to say for yourself?"

Mr Dodds' vocabulary does extend beyond 'I want', 'No' and 'Football!' "This Jew-boy was stealing my fags. He tried to shove me out the window."

Clifford towers above the stringy Mr Dodds. "We'll cut the name-calling, shall we, Mr Dodds? And as we guess Sir Stubborn is of Czech origin, you can think yourself lucky, because throwing people out of windows is part of Czech culture. He meant it as a compliment, didn't you, Josef?"

Josef is rocking to and fro, eyes on the ground. "And don't go into that routine or you'll have to find somebody else to take you to watch Ipswich next season."

Josef stops rocking.

"That's better."

Mr Dodds snaps, "I want my lawyer."

"You had your lawyer yesterday."

"Pen and paper, please. I shall write to the Prime Minister. I have a right to fags."

"Then you *were* stealing fags from Josef, hence his attempt to defenestrate you?"

Defenestrate: hear that, Mrs A? Definitely my new word for the day. It means to cast a person out of a window against his will. Clifford's a crossword freak like you.

Josef is back in front of the telly screen, eyes boring into its blank face. "And you, Josef," says Clifford, "don't think you are going to be let off so lightly. Throwing people out of closed windows just because they pinch a fag is not civilized behaviour. Not in Britain, that is. You should know that by now."

Clifford says he has the rest of his rounds to do. "So as long as you two don't start up the third world war again behind my back, I am leaving Miss Douglas here in charge. She may not look a big muscular girl, but take my word for it, any nonsense from either of you, she'll prove to you what a fine athlete she is."

After quarrels of this kind, it seems, the rivals opt for fresh rivalry: competition as to who can stay up longest. "I'll be back at ten-thirty, Amy, when they'll retire to bed whether they like it or not. Till then, stay here and keep an eye on them."

A terrible silence falls. Amy recognizes it because somewhere in the building, far off, somebody is crying—a child, a grown-up, it is difficult to say. And the crying goes on and on and it makes the silence in this room and the silence outside so clear; like a frost.

It becomes too much to bear. "Josef, I'm Amy. I think you should give Mr Dodds that cigarette he asked for. It will make us all feel better."

"All I wanted was a fag," moans Mr Dodds. He is sallow and sort of hollowed out, yet his balding head still seems too small for the rest of his body. He is a good six inches taller than his friend and enemy.

"One fag, Josef. Are these yours? I guess they must be. There are six in here. You don't have to nod, just promise not to throw us both out of the window. Defenestrate us. That's a new word for me. One cigarette then—for Mr Dodds.

"A peace offering. From a Pacifist and a Buddhist. I'd have thought Buddhists didn't smoke on principle. Okay? Matches?"

"I've got my own matches," says Mr Dodds brusquely. He examines the cigarette as though Josef might have tampered with it. "Huh, all that for one measly fag . . . He hides them under his mattress, Miss. Not supposed to. Against the rules, smoking in bed."

"Listen, Mr Dodds—I don't want to hear anything about that. Especially as Josef has just chosen to let you have a fag instead of throwing you onto the tarmac below."

"They should send him back where he came from. Bloody parasite. Sponging on the National Health."

Amy is beginning to understand. "Then it wasn't just a fag you two were quarrelling over."

"They ought to send him back. He hides fags under his pillows and he's not supposed to. They let him off. They should send him back where he came from."

"And where did he come from?"

"God knows. But they should send him back. He don't talk any . . . And he hides his fags under his pillow. Not right. He'll set us all alight. The whole place'll burn down. I keep telling them. He's a menace. A Communist. Worse still, he's an Israeli spy. Everybody knows that. The doctor knows that, and matron. He's been sent to watch us."

I am surprised at myself. How cool I keep when Mr Dodds pisses all over the floor. Just opens his pyjama bottoms and does it. He must have drunk a keg of Stella. And here is Amy

33

Douglas, not unknown for flying off the occasional handle, cool as a cucumber. "Never mind, Mr Dodds, never mind. You're under pressure."

"My bladder was under pressure."

"No arguing with that."

"In any case, where's the real nurse?"

"Clifford?"

"Betty? She knows when I've the pressure coming on."

"How does she know?"

Yes, cool. Completely ignore him. Take off his slippers (he'd pee-ed all over them); make him stand in it. He says he'll write to the Queen. And order him to bed. "No story for you tonight."

At this, he weeps. Nothing here is predictable. The worst thing is to joke about something: it may be true.

"You're not saying Betty reads you a story?"

"She does more than that."

Amy prefers not to inquire further. "Bed, Mr Dodds."

"I need a wash."

"You want me to wash you?"

He does; and she does. "You stink, Mr Dodds. How often do you wash?"

"Twice a year, on my birthday and at Christmas . . . But you watch out, girl, with him."

"Him?"

"The foreigner. They put him in here because he killed his kids. They refused to be circumcised. He keeps a knife under his pillow."

"Along with his hoard of fags."

"Yes, and there's another thing about him what ought to get him arrested."

"What would that be, Mr Dodds?"

"That case he keeps locked, bottom of his wardrobe. Never

lets nobody near it. Even nurse. And when they bath him he won't let them remove the key from round his neck. He's a Nazi. Take my word for it, girl, he wants deportin'. Huh, fighting over a fag!"

"Maybe he thought you were going for his secret case, Mr Dodds."

"He could 'ave a nuclear bomb in there for all I care."

"Well if I hear it ticking, Mr Dodds, I'll let you know."

Now for the child-murderer, Nazi, Israeli spy and Communist. "You've got a real reputation, Josef. Your friend Mr Dodds says you killed your kids. I don't believe that . . . though you were pretty violent just now. He says that's why you never tell anybody about yourself. Because of your guilt.

"I don't believe that either . . . Do you know what I think? You're afraid. If you just stick with please and thank you, nobody will report you: am I right?"

Why did I say that? Guesswork. But it's pressed something in his head. Josef's gaze for a second shifts from the empty TV screen. "Still, don't think you're the only one. Everybody's afraid—I mean everybody who's ever lost anyone. Or lost themselves, you know what I mean?"

Another flicker of the eye; a recognition. "Yes, I think you do.

"I hope you don't mind me talking to you like this. I lost my parents, you know. They were passengers in this car going along the M25. Heard of that? It's the most dangerous stretch of road since the First World War. Then I went to live with my auntie, who's not actually my real auntie at all. She was kind—so long as I didn't bring home my boyfriend."

The mournful weeping from a distant ward has continued, and until it slips into silence, Amy keeps on talking. Her whole life story pours out like the spring from a mountainside.

"Spen doing what he did—well that's been the last straw, I can tell you. He was brilliant. Everybody said so. I mean, James Joyce—he was reading James Joyce in prison . . . He looked so peaceful.

"But nice kind tolerant old Britain did for him. You're well out of it, Josef. High Lawns is bliss in comparison."

The distant weeping, which had stopped for a few moments, starts up again. "Well, almost bliss . . . Anyway, no more morbid stories. Can you keep a secret, Josef?"

A laugh. "Of course, because you're full of secrets—am I right?"

This time, a nod.

Good. We're communicating. "Well, a small secret. Don't tell anyone, least of all Mr Dodds—I've moved in upstairs. You can come for tea some time, when I've got myself an electric kettle."

He is looking at me. I've beaten the screen. She presses on. "I quite like it here, actually. It's a sanctuary. I think you like it too, Josef. It's a horrible world out there, do you agree?

"I get my meals, same as you. And Mrs Benson thinks they might take me on, as a temp. Pay me, even . . . Mind you, I've only got GCSEs. Though I can swim. I used to race. And when I did, when I competed, left the others ten metres behind, I was somebody. When I didn't, I was nobody.

"You're very trim, Josef. I bet you did sport when you were a boy. Football? They're very keen on it in Czechoslovakia, am I right? Course, personally I'm more into books these days."

She dangles a juicy literary worm. "Now Czechoslovakia— that's where Franz Kafka lived." A pause; a flicker of recognition—no, more than that. "A bit morbid, though—that story about a man turning into a beetle. Poor Gregor Samsa!"

Something is happening. Josef's face seems suddenly to

melt in the glare from the strip light above; melt, go out of shape, and then re-form, almost into a new face.

"One of your favourites, is he, Josef—Franz Kafka? We could—sort of read him together. *The Castle*, what about that? No? Okay, *The Trial* then. My English teacher Mrs Ambler's very keen on him."

Josef suddenly emits one word. Amy does not recognize it, fears it might be a curse. "What was that, Josef?"

"Sveyk!"

"Sveyk? Right." A long pause. Baffled. Sveyk—doesn't sound like a swearword. Josef is reaching out his hand.

"Come. Please!"

Three words! This must have exhausted Josef's usual tally for the year.

"Okay."

Upstairs, to his room, head nodding now, vigorously. Josef switches on the light, goes to a set of drawers, opens the top one.

Amy waits by the door. "Sveyk." She practises it aloud. Does it mean 'bedroom' or 'drawer' or perhaps even 'secret case'?

Josef produces a fat paperback with a flash of yellow on the cover. He holds it up. "Sveyk."

At last. "He's the author?" She receives the book. She reads out the title. "*The Good Soldier Sveyk* by Jaroslav Ha—sek."

"Hashek!" replies Josef, correcting Amy's pronunciation.

Eyes meeting, eyes aglow now.

On the cover, an officer in a blue uniform is sitting down and smoking a fag. Coming through the door, saluting, is a plump soldier with a stubble beard and a big grin. "Sveyk?"

Amy points, Josef nods. She turns to the back cover and reads: "*The Good Soldier Sveyk and His Fortunes in the World War* . . . it says here that it's the 'classic novel of the "little man" fighting officialdom and bureaucracy with the only weapons available to him—passive resistance, subterfuge, native wit and dumb insolence'."

Dumb insolence, eh? Amy gazes across at her new friend. All she says is, "Sveyk!"

Josef nods again, and now he smiles. "Sveyk!"

"And you want me to read this to you?" She examines the volume which has suddenly brought her close to this old man full of dumb insolence. "Seven hundred and fifty-two pages, Josef—that'll take us a lifetime!"

Another nod. No sweat. She flicks through the pages, pauses at Chapter Four: *Sveyk Thrown out of the Lunatic Asylum*. She looks up but does not speak, then turns to the opening page.

She reads out the first few lines:

> *'And so they've killed Grand Duke Ferdinand,' said the charwoman to Mr Sveyk, who had left military service years before, after being finally certified by an army medical board as an imbecile, and now lived by selling dogs—ugly, mongrel monstrosities, whose pedigrees he forged.*
>
> *Apart from this occupation he suffered from rheumatism and was at this very moment rubbing his knees with Elliman's embrocation . . .*

Amy's turn to nod. "It looks as though it might give us a laugh or two."

Josef is beaming. All at once Amy begins to feel good. She closes the book.

"Sveyk!" says the old man.

"Sveyk!" repeats Amy Douglas, little realizing how this one word will change her life.

Chapter Four

"It's really quite remarkable, JP—the progress Amy has made with our Sir Stubborn over the past few weeks."

"Sir Stubborn? Now Sylvia, you know it's a house rule—"

"Well Josef Kastov isn't his real name either, is it, JP?"

"You know as well as I do, Sylvia, that Josef's documents were misplaced in transit to High Lawns. And after twenty years or more it's rather too long to hope they'll ever turn up. However, it is good news that he has found his tongue and that Amy is making progress with him."

"Well, the rest of us'll have to go on making do with please and thank you—which is progress. But Amy has the gift. He chats to her. She reads to him. Every night. Serious books—I was quite amazed."

"And you wish to take her on the staff as a temp?"

"They're all fond of her. Except Mr Dodds who thinks she is a spy from the Ministry of Social Security. What I particularly wanted to mention is this extraordinary discovery she has made about our Josef—he is a poet!"

"A wordless poet?"

"Not at all. Amy was dusting out his locker, remembering not to touch his precious case, and found a folder full of poems. In Czech, though a few lines here and there are in English. Would you believe it?"

"It could all be gobbledegook, Sylvia."

"That's what Betty the night nurse thought it was. She says she's chucked out loads of his stuff."

"Good grief, then let's hope for the sake of posterity that it really is gobbledegook. Still, from now on, be careful to keep everything our Josef writes in a folder."

"Amy's already doing that. She's brought him pads of paper and given him a nice silver propelling pencil that belonged to her father. Josef won't write with anything else now . . . Is something the matter, JP?"

"I'm just a little afraid that in her youthful enthusiasm Amy might be putting ideas into Josef's head. It is also a rule of the house not to over-excite our patients."

JP is uncharacteristically severe. "I think you will have to have a quiet word with the girl, Sylvia. Her own hopes have been somewhat dashed of late. If she transfers them to Josef . . . well, you understand."

"A relapse?"

"Exactly. If Amy is to remain with us, she must have that danger spelt out to her. Poems or not, gobbledegook or not, Josef is too far gone ever to look beyond these walls."

"Father Havran? A young girl has called to see you. She says she wrote to you, sent you some poems."

"Please show her in. Amy? Take a seat."

"I never realized there was a Czech church in London, Father."

"The church in exile—but not any longer. Our country is free once more and soon we shall pack up our troubles and return." Father Havran is full of cold. He has a box of tissues beside him; indeed everything around him is in boxes. "Hay fever," he grunts apologetically, issuing a trumpet blast into two handfuls of tissues.

"Dust mites," decides Amy. "I read in the paper that they

multiply by ten million a second." She notices above Father Havran's desk a framed photograph of the president of the Czech republic, poet and playwright Vaclav Havel.

She points at the picture. "I wish we had a poet and a playwright for a prime minister. Is he a friend of yours, Father?"

The priest takes another turn at the trumpet. "So sorry . . . Yes, we met in jail. He was coming in when I was going out. Then the next time I was going in, he was coming out. It's been that sort of country."

"And now he's president."

"And I've got ten million dust mites in my nose . . . Now, these poems, Amy."

"Tell me they're not gobbledegook."

"On the contrary, they are amazing. They are the work of a writer of immense talent. I would very much like to send them to a literary friend of mine, a publisher in Prague.

"But who on earth is this mysterious Czech poet? You gave me so little information in your letter. I mean, for a start, you only call him Josef."

"That's because we know nothing about him, not even his surname. So he goes down on the forms as Kastov."

"Ah, somebody's little joke—'Josef K'. I doubt if you'll have come across the novels of Franz Kafka, Amy, but—"

"Josef K's the poor old land assessor in *The Castle*, always waiting for his summons to the Castle, yet it never comes."

Father Havran is impressed. "And a Josef K also appears in *The Trial*—not a very agreeable book. Well, well, young lady!"

"Josef prefers me to read him *The Good Soldier Sveyk*. It's a laugh, Sveyk getting up the nose of everybody in authority."

Father Havran smiles. "There is a Sveyk in all of us."

Amy goes on, "I've been reading everything I can about

41

Prague. Josef's from there, like Sveyk. He used to go to the same pub. When he's feeling up to it, we're going back. A little holiday. He wants to stand on Charles Bridge and listen to the jazz players. It's his dream. But JP mustn't find out, not just yet."

"JP?"

"Dr Parrish. He's in charge at High Lawns. To be honest, he'd have kittens if he knew I was here—pushing things . . . But Father, I'd like you to come and visit Josef. Talk to him in his own language. I'm sure that would help."

Father Havran grabs more tissues yet this time holds back a sneeze. "Twenty years in such an institution. Josef must have been terribly afraid."

Amy waits. She has her own theories. "Yes?"

"Of what they would do to him if they caught up with him."

"The secret police—the StB?"

"I see you've been doing your homework, Amy."

"But Father, what harm could a poet do them?"

"Make people laugh at them, perhaps . . . I guess he must have escaped when the Russian tanks rolled into Prague."

"1968?"

Father Havran looks pleased that somebody knows a bit of Czech history. "Yes, and after that people who spoke out of turn, disagreed—or were even suspected of thinking their own thoughts were likely to end up in a freezing cell. Any children they had would never get beyond secondary school. There'd be no jobs, no rights at all! As far as the government was concerned, such people ceased to exist.

"Oh yes, there'd be plenty of reasons for escape in those days."

"Well Josef certainly ceased to exist . . . But why end up at High Lawns, Father? After all, you didn't."

"Perhaps your Josef is a man of little faith, Amy." A huge sneeze rescues Amy from a short sermon on How Faith Sees You Through.

Perhaps I should have mentioned that Josef is Jewish. "Will you come and see him, Father?"

"I shall."

"And the poems?"

"I will take them with me to Prague. In the meantime, perhaps you can try to persuade him to tell us his real name."

"Everybody wants me to find out about him—but that's the trouble. As soon as I ask Josef about himself, we're back to the TV gaze. He'll chat about Prague, but nothing else. He just says, 'I not have past'."

"You know, Josef, it's all take on your part. You want us to look after you. You want me to read to you. You want me to teach you to swim. Well I may not be here much longer. Something has happened. I've been in a little bit of trouble again. And anyway, I've a life to live. Do you understand? I've had enough of asylum.

"On the other hand, I like you. But why wouldn't you see Father Havran?"

Off Josef went with one of his skits:

> *Havran the raven*
> *Havran the raven*
> *The raven called Havran*
> *Risks Josef's safe haven.*

"No, he's working wonders on your behalf, Josef. Clifford thinks you refused to see him because he's a Catholic and you're Jewish. But I think you're just scared of meeting your countryman.

"Listen, if you don't speak to him, he'll be gone for good . . . Back to your beloved Prague. I've been reading up about it—your whole country.

"The nightmare's over. There aren't any more Russian tanks. No more night arrests. No political prisoners. Is that what you were—and escaped?"

Nothing. And Amy is feeling bad about herself. No wonder he clams up with all these questions. Do I leave it there? No. "I've been reading about the famous Jewish cemetery in Prague, Josef. Weird—all those thousands of tombstones, three layers deep. Were any of your relatives buried there?"

I think I get a reaction. "I've been wondering, about the Nazis, how they transported thousands of kids from their homes. Jewish kids. You are old enough to remember that, Josef, aren't you?"

A shake of the head, eyes down, the past wiped away.

This is cruel, but why won't he budge?

Father Havran: "Josef's poetry gives nothing away about his identity. It's masterly but also a feat of disguise—except for one little skit, very characteristic of light-hearted Czech verse.

"Here, I've translated it. What do you think? It's a sort of guided tour of the pubs of Prague."

She treasures the lines because they are a tease, full of fun, which is what Josef must have once been.

Sylvia Benson catches Amy dreaming. "Have you seen Josef, Amy? He's gone missing again. He's really becoming a pain."

"I left him playing chess with Mr Dodds."

"Yes, and Mr Dodds apparently accused him of being a Jewish cheat."

"I'll search the grounds."

"Good, Clifford is scouring the building."

Thirty acres, much of it woodland. That bloody Dodds. He ought to be locked away. Of course, he *is* locked away. We're all locked away.

Josef isn't under his favourite copper beech tree. It is getting too cool for sitting out. Can I stand an autumn and then winter in this place? Amy makes for the greenhouses where Josef cultivates his own patch, growing tomatoes tiny as marbles, but delicious.

Not here, so round to the herb garden and the stone bench where all summer Amy has read to her friend the adventures of *The Good Soldier Sveyk*.

She calls, "Sveyk?—orders from the Colonel. Report to barracks at once!"

Was your wise old grandad also a pest sometimes, Mrs A? Well, Josef, you're not my grandad and I'm wondering just why I'm wasting my youth giving out and getting nothing back.

Trouble is, when I'm with my own kind, there's trouble. Nothing but aggro. Like Saturday. I reckon the cops will be on to JP this very minute.

Then it'll be adios AD.

If you could see me now, Spen, you'd probably decide you took the easy way out. Still, not everything's gloom and doom. Amy Douglas has dug up a poet. Who may even be a great poet.

Yes, Mrs A, I'm out here and I'm making a bit of history.

The main gate is ajar and all at once she hears him laughing. He has pushed the gate to and is now racing back up the drive, zig-zagging, waving his arms about.

For some reason he counts this a great victory. He dodges into the trees, leaping up and down like a dwarf wearing red-hot shoes. And he's chanting:

Amy's slick
And Amy's quick
But Josef's slicker
And Josef's quicker.

"Is it your birthday, Josef?"

Dodds is mad
And Dodds is bad
But Josef's madder
And Josef's badder.

He is puffed out, but there's a flush in his face and his eyes are brighter than Amy's ever seen them. It must be the autumn air. "Is this what they get up to in Prague at this time of year, Josef? Play hide and seek in the Old Town?"

He is away, darting, feet hardly touching the ground; for an old codger, stiff as a board, his lungs probably deep black with cigarette smoke, he's got real athlete potential.

"I think you must have got good news. A letter, perhaps?" Always asking that. He gets no letters. No one writes to somebody called Kastov. "Your poems are to be published?"

"Maybe."

Maybe means for certain. "That's wonderful—by Josef K or Josef X?"

"Guess, Milacku!" This means, in Czech, 'Dear One' or 'Sweetheart'; it's out of Sveyk, and it makes Amy feel good when he uses it.

Milacku!

They sit on a bench under the great willow. He points. Geese are flying south. "Isn't it time you and me took wing, Josef? We could sit in the famous old Chalice, drink a pint

46

of the best lager in the world and you could recite your poems while I collected our rent money in a hat. How about it—real escape, not dodging round the lupins."

Mention of The Chalice plunges him in to thought.

She goes for more names—anything to shift him into gear. "Then we'll go to a concert in Smetana Hall or maybe to see one of Havel's plays at the Theatre on the Balustrade."

I know I am getting through, but Josef is shaking his head. "Too cold."

"Not if we wrap up. We'll feed the seagulls on the River Vltava, then back to The Chalice for a double slivovice."

Another shake of the head, but this time accompanied by a smile. "Slivovice? No."

"What then?"

"Bechers. Is stronger!"

I'm stirring him, but I'm also tempting myself. All the places I mention, for his benefit, are now beginning to glow in my own mind. I've seen nothing, been nowhere; yet now I *know* where I want to go.

Ticket to Prague: that's what I'm after. Ticket to the City of Gold. I want to see the spires and the pinnacles rising out of the river mist.

"Then shake a leg for my sake, Josef. I want to go to Golden Lane, to the house Kafka lived in below the castle. And the pink tank—"

"The pink tank?"

"Yes, some students—to annoy the Russians. Painted a tank bright pink! It was in the paper.

"Defiance, Josef!"

He stares at Amy, tilts his head as he always does when he is caught between thoughts. He wags his finger at her as most of her teachers used to do.

True, I'm a sad spectacle these days. For a second I think

47

he is sorry for me. Maybe for the first time in years he is looking at life from somebody else's point of view.

He raises his hand, ever so frailly, to her face. She does not pull back, as she usually would when approached by an uninvited touch. He brushes a few stray hairs from her cheek.

It is something my mum did; and all at once I'm flooded with remembrances.

"Poor Milacku!" His head tilts further, like a bird's, listening. I don't realize there's a tear on my cheek. He lifts it off with the side of his forefinger.

He begins to nod. His eyes are bright. They suddenly seem to encompass the future. In another moment, everything might have been decided, but Clifford comes striding through the trees and the spell is broken.

"There you are, you old reprobate!"

But the message Clifford brings is for Amy. JP wishes to see her. "As a matter of urgency, he said."

Josef is away, heading for the birchwood, half running, half skipping:

> *Fire, burn; and caldron bubble,*
> *Milacku's set for double trouble.*

Amy goes to the house alone. Poor Milacku, yes. On her way to execution.

"JP? You wanted to see me."

"Come in, Miss Douglas. Please sit down. I am afraid neither of us is going to enjoy what I have to say to you."

The sins of Amy Douglas are to be laid out before her. "I will deal with the matter of the police later, Amy."

No more AD.

First, there is the matter of her visit to the hospital in London. "Did you or did you not make enquiries about

48

Josef without informing either myself or Mrs Benson?"

"It was on my day off."

"You drew a blank, I believe."

"They don't hold records for more than a few months."

"But they gave you the name of a retired hospital porter who might just have remembered Josef. Correct?"

"Yes, Doctor."

No more JP.

"Well? Did he remember Josef?"

"He remembered a photograph—in the *Daily Mirror*. Looked like Josef."

"What was the picture about?"

"Was it so wrong, Dr Parrish, to—"

"Just tell me about the photograph. Was there a name?"

"He didn't have the picture any longer."

"But you have, Amy—do you not?"

"I don't know what you mean, Doctor."

"I think you do. A week ago, on your day off, you went to London again, this time to the national newspaper archives in Colindale. You were permitted to look up papers published in 1968, the year the Russians invaded Czechoslovakia—am I right? After all, Amy, you gave them our address."

Nothing for it but to nod, and keep on nodding.

"As soon as you had departed the archive, an official discovered you had torn out a page from the *Mirror* dated August 1968. A criminal offence, Amy.

"Then there is the matter of your being arrested with your friend Trish at the Ecstasy party in Clacton on Saturday night."

"It wasn't an E-do at all. Just a disco."

"Not what the police claim."

"I thought you were asking about Josef's picture. It's him, I'm sure. In Wenceslas Square . . . Prague, that is. And there's a young boy on his shoulder—possibly his son. Wearing a Basque cap and holding up a placard—"

"Miss Douglas, I don't—"

"But it's important, Doctor. The placard says, in English, TELL ME THE TRUTH SO I WON'T HAVE TO SEARCH FOR IT WHEN I GROW UP. That boy will be grown up now—and he'll want to know the truth about his father."

Amy has forgotten all about the cops and her arrest; all about how she should have kept her trap shut and let the boys in blue go on insulting Trish.

Dr Parrish has not forgotten. "More pressing, Amy, than detective work going back over twenty years, is the fact that the archive intends to sue you. And on the other matter, the police are charging you with assault."

"Assault? I never touched them."

"But you abused them, using obscenities."

A silence. Amy cannot bear Dr Parrish staring at her like this, hurt rather than angry; with 'I've been let down' written all over his face.

She is resigned. "Is that it, then?"

But Dr Parrish hasn't finished. "All those things I can forgive, Amy. I am not totally blind to the behaviour of policemen when they break up parties. I could even understand how that picture of Josef and the boy meant so much to you that you ripped it out and stole it."

He pauses, curious. "You say there was no name? A pity. You still have the picture?"

A reluctant nod: it's stuck up over the bath next to her Freddy Mercury poster.

"We will photocopy the page before you return it personally to the curator of the archive. Bearing with it your abject apologies. Understand?"

"Yes, Doctor."

50

Another silence. "But you see, Amy, the most serious charge against you is what you are trying to do to Josef. He has been here too long for what you want of him. Too institutionalized. He is beyond rescue. The outside world holds terrors for him which I doubt any of us could begin to comprehend."

"He is a poet, Doctor. Perhaps a great poet. He is finding himself again."

"And you are a teenager, full of impossible dreams."

Dr Parrish had begun the interview with every intention of dismissing Amy Douglas instantly. 'Forthwith!' as he had said to Sylvia Benson. But he had never dismissed anyone from his employ. He hadn't the words, perhaps not the courage.

And Amy Douglas appealed to something within him, something that had, in his adult years, his growing-old years, all but faded: a spark of hope; of faith, even.

Could she be right?

He is about to reserve judgment concerning Amy's future at High Lawns when the phone rings. As he listens to the caller, Dr Parrish is annoyed at his train of thought being interrupted. Then his face passes through different moods, from surprise to suspicion and then to apprehension. "Excuse me for a moment."

The doctor puts his hand over the mouthpiece. "This, Amy, is the BBC. A documentary film maker by the name of Alan Francis. It seems he wishes to make a short film about Josef. And I am wondering just how he found out about him."

For the very first time during her interrogation, Amy Douglas is completely innocent of the charge.

But she is excited. The BBC! Hear that, Josef? "Not me, Doctor. Honestly. Not me."

Dr Parrish returns to his caller. He is not finding it easy to conceal his own excitement.

The BBC, calling High Lawns!

"Well, yes, Mr Francis. We consider Josef a poet of real merit. But I would have to insist on safeguards. Under no circumstances must he be over-excited. And naturally he would have to be consulted before any agreement to film took place."

Dr Parrish replaces the phone. As if, in the next few moments, he were about to be interviewed on camera, he instinctively straightens his tie.

"They seem to know Josef's name already," he says, dazed by the rush of events. "In future, we must no longer call him Josef Kastov. He is Josef Sabata, a poet who escaped from a cultural delegation to Britain in 1973, but who was reported killed in a road accident soon afterwards."

Dr Parrish stands up. "Well I never! Television cameras at High Lawns. They will of course be interested in the care we lavish on our patients. And in our success-rate in rehabilitation.

"Perhaps we hide our light under a bushel a little too much." JP's mind has strayed far from concerns about stolen press photographs, angry archivists and allegedly assaulted police officers. High Lawns on TV!

He stares at Amy. "Shouldn't you be on duty, AD?"

Chapter Five

"Josef, you're famous again."

Father Havran has sent Amy two newspapers. They must have got a picture from somewhere because Josef is on the front page of a Czech paper, one of their nationals—*Svobodne Slovo*; and there's this other paper, in English—*Prague News*, which earns Amy's prize for a winning headline:

BACK FROM THE DEAD

Slovak poet of 60s surfaces in English Nursing Home. Poems to be published simultaneously in Czech, German and English.

PLANS FOR MEDAL CEREMONY

The great mystery of the whereabouts of one of Slovakia's finest young poets of the 1960s, Josef Sabata, has at last been solved: Josef K. (for Kastov) as they called him, has been living in a place of refuge since the Russian tanks destroyed the Prague Spring of Liberty in 1968. At one time a friend of Vaclav Havel, playwright and dissident, and now President of the Republic, Sabata is thought to have died in the years of repression which followed the period of so-called Normalization.

Some sources thought he had died in prison, others that he had attempted to escape and been shot. Others believe he was smuggled out of the country and went to Canada, where he died.

There are indeed those here in Prague who refuse to believe that the Josef K. who has turned up in England is the real Josef Sabata at all. One source, close to the Dissident movement throughout the 1970s and 80s told us: "We should greet this resurrection of a great Slovak poet with caution, especially as Sabata was suspected at the time of collaboration with the Communist dictatorship.

"If he returns to Czechoslovakia his credentials will have to be scrutinized most carefully. However, if Sabata really was a collaborator, his knowledge of other collaborators in the field of the arts might be of vital importance in the lustration process."

There we go again, Mrs A: a new word for the day. Apparently lustration is all the rage over there. I guess you'll know what it means. Sort of purification. By sacrifice. They're shining the torch on a lot of dark corners. Sniffing out the old traitors and shouting their names from the rooftops.

Sounds dicey to me. What if they get it wrong? If Josef doesn't go to Prague after all the publicity, they'll take it as an admission of guilt.

"And now you too are famous, Milacku!" Josef in good spirits after Amy's second appearance in court. "We are both wicked people—like we always wanted to be."

From Amy, a grin; but very upset. "Infamous is the word, Josef."

Another newspaper, this time closer to home, with Amy

Douglas as the bad fairy. Lustration isn't mentioned, Amy thinks, because it has too many syllables.

The tabloid headline reads: DOTTY POET'S PAL CALLS COPS WHITE PRATS. And underneath: *Czech émigré wordsmith speaks up for girl who nursed him back to sanity.*

It had been an exciting month and a sad one; exciting because Alan Francis and his BBC film crew came to High Lawns and took the first footage of their documentary on Josef; sad because Amy's auntie died in the nursing home.

Up until her final illness, Auntie had refused to see Amy when she tried to visit her. Eventually, robbed of sight, speech and comprehension, she clutched Amy's hand so tightly it was hard to gain her release when visiting time was over.

"I'm on duty, Auntie. My job. Just what you wanted for me. Dad and Mum would have been proud. Please be proud of me too!"

At the graveside there had been all that was left of Auntie's world: the assistant matron of the nursing home, Amy and Evie—still with her mind on the stolen kimono. Present but apart was Amy's childhood friend Trish, who had come out of friendship for Amy and brought a beautiful bouquet from her father's grocery emporium.

The solicitor was to announce that Amy Douglas had been left the sum of £1573 in her aunt's will.

She had gone out the same day and put down a deposit for two tickets to Prague.

"Madam, the exact words employed by the accused to the arresting officers as they went about their duty, were: 'Shove off, you white prats'."

"That's not true!" interrupts Amy, banging the polished

oak rail in front of her. "I said, 'Why don't you pick on somebody your own size?'"

Chairing the magistrates is a lady who is also a governor of Amy's old school. She senses that she has encountered this brash young woman before, but cannot quite place her. "Did you or did you not use the term 'White Prats'?"

The courtroom is full. On the night of the party, described by a local paper as X FOR ESSEX MEETING X FOR ECSTASY, there had been sixty-five arrests. There are twenty-five due for trial today, including Amy and Trish—though at no time during the altercation with the police had Trish so much as opened her mouth.

Except to breathe, that is.

Squashed into the public gallery are relatives and friends, including Sylvia Benson, accompanying Josef who had insisted on being present. Equally resolved to come along was Mr Dodds, sworn to be on his best behaviour. "I know all about courts," he said. "I've spent half my life in them."

The lady magistrate, to be addressed as Madam, had made it clear from the beginning that she was not in a smiling mood: "There is a spirit of levity in this court which is entirely inappropriate considering the seriousness of the allegations."

The comment was a response to someone throwing a streamer across the court as the two magistrates took their places at the bench, and causing howls of mirth among teenage friends of the accused.

"I blame the schools," the male magistrate, to be addressed as Sir, murmured to the court clerk.

Did Miss Douglas wish to say anything in her defence?

"I do . . . I am sorry I called the officers White Prats. But it has not been reported here what the officers called my friend Trish. Humbly begging the court's pardon . . ."

Here Amy glances up at the public gallery and Josef: a

56

private joke between them—for the Good Soldier Sveyk always addressed his superiors in this way; 'Humbly reporting, Sir' and then he would go on and tell a meandering story that would somehow excuse him of his folly and make his listener stamping mad.

"Humbly begging the court's pardon, there is a little bit of this story which has not been told: who started the verbal fireworks in the first place."

"Just what was said to your friend?" Madam feels a flicker of sympathy and interest.

"Well, I shall have to go back a little in history."

But not that much interest: "Pray keep it brief."

Sir is glancing at his watch. He has a lunch appointment. He forgets that it is his duty to speak through the chair. "Just tell us, Miss, what the officers are alleged to have said to your friend."

"I'd prefer to write it down on paper, Sir, if you don't mind. They are . . ." Amy had been saving up these words all her life, it seemed: "Scurrilous, if not maledicent."

"I beg your pardon?" Giggles stir the court. 'Scurrilous', yes, the magistrates could make sense of that; but 'maledicent'—was this a new word game?

Madam whispers for a moment with Sir, then treats Amy to the beginning of a smile. "I think we have been around long enough not to be shocked, Miss Douglas. Proceed!"

"Very well, Your Honours. The officers maledicently said to my friend, 'Stir your ass, you Black Bitch or you'll get curried truncheon up your—'"

"Silence in court!" bellows the court clerk.

"I was only saying . . ." Amy appeals to Madam who has muttered, "Disgraceful!" "I agree with you entirely—it was disgraceful. What's more, if you'll excuse me saying, it was a very uncouth, boorish and scurrilous thing to say to a girl whose grandmother was at that very moment dying in a National Health Service hospital corridor while awaiting treatment."

Sir rocks back in his chair and throws up his hands. "You'll be blaming the government next!"

As Sir has grown hot, Madam has found it difficult to hold back a grin; this spreads out of control when Amy says, "Madam, begging your pardon, I would like to read a passage from Shakespeare—"

"Shakespeare?" intrudes Sir. "What has he got to do with verbal assault?"

"Shakespeare," responds the accused, "wrote the most wonderful speech ever spoken in a court of law."

Sir is reluctant to be seen slagging off the nation's greatest poet in public. On the other hand, he is five minutes late for his lunch appointment. "What is this speech about?"

"A pound of flesh, your Honour. You see—"

"A pound of *what*?"

Madam lays her hand lightly on her colleague's arm. Perhaps this is the moment she has waited for all her life. She faces the court, turns her gaze up to the gallery, and recites:

> *The quality of mercy is not strain'd*
> *It droppeth as the gentle rain from heaven*
> *Upon the place beneath. It is twice blessed . . .*

Amy falls for the words and, like Madam, forgets who she is and where she is. She takes up the lines from the magistrate:

> *It blesses him that gives and him that takes.*
> *'Tis mightiest in the mightiest; it becomes*
> *The throned monarch better than his crown . . .*

Josef is on his feet, leading applause. Something has happened here. Only Sir manages to keep his head. His own mercy severely strained, he taps his watch under Madam's nose: result, for Amy, a fine of fifty pounds in sterling, not in flesh; to be paid in weekly instalments of five, ten or fifteen.

Sir has the last word, for Madam is still beguiled by the words of Portia in *The Merchant of Venice*: "And think yourself lucky, Douglas, you're not being charged with wasting court time . . . Next criminal, please!"

So far so good, but outside the courtroom, with Josef on Amy's arm now, not so good: blinding flashes from a dozen cameras.

"Sir?" To Josef. "Can you tell us what you think about British justice compared to how you suffered at the hands of your Communist jailers?"

The Press, feels Amy, is as bad as Svejk: they say Sir and then put the boot in. She takes command. "No questions, thank you."

Orders from Mrs Benson who has taken Mr Dodds off because of his bladder trouble. And good sense. "We don't want Josef regressing now the plane ticket has been booked and paid for."

How come all these pressmen; to a little provincial courtcase? Who put them on to the story?

"Sir, what do you think of your young friend here—calling the police White Prats?"

"Just let us through, please. Mr Sabata has to return home."

"Is it true the Czech government is paying all his expenses?"

"What sort of medal is he going to get?"

"Does he take sugar?"

A laugh all round; and Amy has to join in. "He likes the occasional fag."

"Funded by the British taxpayer?"

"Who's been footing the bills for the past twenty years, Amy?"

Who gave them permission to call me Amy?

Josef keeps on smiling. He is probably not taking anything in. Something on his mind.

"Do you read bedtime stories to him at night, Amy?"

"Is it true Joe was in jail with Vaclav Havel and they didn't see eye to eye?"

"Come on, Lovely, give us some facts."

"I'm sorry. We really must—"

And then the question that makes Amy's stomach churn. "What's this about his case of secret documents?"

This bit of information isn't common knowledge. Tomorrow the world will know about it. "Documents?"

"Keeps the key round his neck, even when he's having his bath. Right, Josef?"

"Got the key, Joe? What's in that case, Joe?"

Amy is moving Josef along, down the steps, into the crowd. Who told them? She makes one confident guess: thanks, Mr Dodds; but who did Mr Dodds tell?

Thanks, Alan Francis; been chatting to your press pals, have you? Not a friend in the camp after all.

"No comment!"

"Will you pose in your bikini for us, Amy?"

She is tall. She brushes the reporters and cameramen aside. "Piss off, the lot of you."

Josef seems dazed, but also reluctant to go at Amy's pace. Then he stops. He puts up his hand as if begging an audience's silence before addressing them.

He recites:

> *Blue hats, white prats;*
> *White hats, blue prats.*
> *Smacks for Blacks*
> *Whippo gypo, stew the Jew.*
> *Tears for queers when cops go pop.*
> *Into the pot you pressmen stir*
> *Fears and leers and spleen of cur.*
> *Blue hats, white prats*
> *Beware the state that lets them mate*
> *With sewer rats.*

This is too much even for hard-nosed reporters who love a punchy line. There is a clamour of protest as Amy ushers Josef out of the crowd. The reporters do not pursue them: they already have their story.

Words are having a ball.

There's salt in the air from a sea wind and Josef gets an ocean of a hug from Amy. "Maledicent, Josef, definitely maledicent. The Good Soldier would have been proud of us!"

By the next day High Lawns has become the most famous hospital for mental patients in Britain. One of its trainee nurses is reported as telling the gentlemen of the press to 'Piss off!' while a guest of the nation, 'living off the fat of the British taxpayer', has described them as 'sewer rats'.

Amy Douglas has yet another charge to answer—before Dr Parrish, profoundly shocked and looking unusually pale and sunken. "Honestly, Doctor, I don't remember Josef giving the press the V-sign. Unless he was pretending to be Winston Churchill."

Not a good word can be read in any of the papers (considering that the so-called serious press were not represented at the event and do not carry the story).

"It is a disaster. A calamitous disaster! All our careful work over the years—goes up in smoke."

Sylvia Benson is not so sure. "They say there's no such thing as bad publicity, JP."

"Are you joking, Sylvia? Do you realize what Josef's words have done? To call the press sewer rats?"

"Well, aren't they?"

"Most of them, but you don't tell them that to their face."

Amy wants to say, "Why not, if it's true?" But her mouth has got her into more than enough trouble lately.

"Amy, you were under instructions, under oath indeed, to keep a low profile on things. Not to rock the boat. That was our bargain. Quite the reverse has occurred. You have brought this institution into disrepute. Your problem, young lady, is that you have respect for nothing and nobody."

"I respect Josef."

"Then see the harm you have done to him. His own future in this home is at risk. And at least two papers are calling for his extradition. Do you know what that word means, seeing you're so full of them?"

Amy nods. She had read it in the paper. She's looked it up in the dictionary. "They're bluffing."

"Oh, are they? Well let me tell you this—if Josef can't prove that he is in danger of his life and liberty should he return to Czechoslovakia, there'll be no justification for keeping him here."

Mrs Benson is not happy about this. "Josef is unwell, JP. He cannot cope with life outside of these gates, never mind in a country he's not visited in twenty years."

"If our poet steps on that plane, Sylvia, immigration won't let him back in. Not with the papers gunning for him. Sewer rats! I'm half convinced the press has a point. He's become a bit of a menace."

Amy can hold back no longer. "How can you say that? After all, he was just as hard on the cops: *tears for queers when cops go pop*—"

"And I'm supposed to be pleased about that?"

"Is that what you want, JP?" Amy is shouting now.

"Don't call me that!"

"Dr Parrish, then. Is that what you want, for Josef to return to his silence, his blank telly screen?"

"Of course not."

"Cabbage—you want him to be a cabbage again."

"Nonsense. But under your influence he has slid to the other extreme."

"My influence?"

"Yes, your influence. Didn't the magistrate comment on it—the way you were a bad influence on that Asian friend of yours? Didn't her parents agree with him? Similarly with Josef."

"You object to Josef's conduct because—because he's become a rebel?" Amy speaks the word with respect.

"Exactly!" Dr Parrish thinks of the word with horror. "What I find hard to forgive is Josef's lack of gratitude for what we—no, the country, has done for him."

The tears sting at the corners of Amy's eyes. "Have you forgotten why he spoke those lines? He spoke them for me, to defend me. He spoke out for me when nobody else in this world would."

Sylvia Benson nods. "I'd say that was gratitude, Amy."

"No," barks back Amy. "Friendship!"

She finds Josef down by the empty swimming pool. He is in his new overcoat, bought for the journey to Prague. He is very proud of the leather collar and the leather pocket buttons. "A poet's coat," he had said.

Dr Parrish had protested about the expenditure until Amy assured him she had bought the coat with money from her aunt's will. That and the birch-grey suit and black brogue shoes.

But most poetic of all, in Amy's view—and Josef had seemed willing to go along with the new image she was creating for him—was the black felt trilby with extra-wide brim.

The final touch had been a scarlet wool scarf. "Now you look like that poster I bought for your room—the Toulouse-Lautrec," she had said.

"How are you feeling, Josef?"

"Perfect, Milacku."

"No worries?"

"I like it."

"Like it?"

Josef smiles. "Yes—being in bother again!"

Chapter Six

It was to be a mixed send-off. Mr Dodds, in Amy's view, kind of summed everything up. "Don't ever come back," he warned Josef; and in the next breath he said, "Bring me some of that Czech beer. It's the best in the West."

Dr Parrish drove them to the airport. Somewhere along here, Amy Douglas had become an orphan. I'd have liked to put some roses at the spot, but I'd have been knocked down doing it.

Somewhere around here: hello, Mum, hello, Dad. We're off to Prague, the golden city. I know how beautiful it is because Josef has told me all about it. Once, you couldn't get a word out of him, now he never stops talking—though he's scared of the traffic at the moment.

How've I been? Bad, but improving. Yesterday I was so happy, and then this letter came. For some reason Josef can't bring himself to read his mail. A good thing because this little hand-grenade has depressed me ever since I opened it.

No name, of course, and written in capitals. It warns Josef not to go to Prague. Like the rest of *Homo sapiens*, the writer has read about Josef's very special case.

He's got it with him now.

"It would be a lot safer to leave your case here at High Lawns, Josef."

No: where Joe goes, the case goes. I've started calling it Pandora, after Pandora's Box: when opened, all the evils of the world fly out.

It worries me, Pandora. And it's intrigued the press. "Unless," the note says, "you burn the case, you will burn in hell."

One paper has published an article on Josef Sabata linking the contents of the case with Russia's invasion of Czechoslovakia in '68. Of course, of course!—missing documents, got to be: identifying the traitors who conspired with the KGB to plan the attack and occupation.

The article concludes: *Such persons have the blood of their countrymen on their hands—and may still hold positions of power and influence in Czechoslovakia.*

Maybe I should have told JP about the letter. No—he'd only have panicked and tried to postpone the trip. Okay, let's both burn in hell. But before that we're going for gold. The medal ceremony in Hradcany Castle is going to be *my* treat too.

I want to see Vaclav Havel shake hands with my Josef.

Father Havran is at Heathrow's Terminal 2 to greet the distinguished Slovak poet, Josef Sabata. The priest looks deathly. "I've the flu," he confesses. "So sorry." He needs a supporting hand more than Josef.

In fact Josef takes his other arm. "And I suffer from air sickness."

Out of his own money, Josef buys Father Havran a cup of freshly crushed orange juice. He speaks to him in Czech, makes the priest smile. "No," replies Havran in English, "whatever the Communists did to our country, they did not spoil the beer, Josef."

The surprise is the arrival of Alan Francis and his film crew—Eddie the cameraman, Jamie the sound recordist and

Sabrina, Alan's personal assistant (the one, Amy has decided, who does all the work).

"You're a bastard!" This is said so loudly a dozen passengers stare at the girl with one hand on her hip, the other pointing in accusation at a face some of them just faintly recognize.

"Isn't that . . . ?"

"Well whoever he is, he's in for it!"

At first Amy and Alan had got on well. She classified him as a perpetual firework, bursting with energy and zest, sparkling with ideas, wild comments and occasional wit. Ample compensation, she decided, for him being squat, balding, over forty and prone to excessive sweat.

In the pub after the first shooting of the documentary, Alan impressed by buying all the drinks, including one for Mr Dodds who claimed to have been Alfred Hitchcock before his illness.

Then Alan had ruined things with Amy by coming on strong: "My peculiar preference, Amy, is for tall blondes with legs exactly the curvature of yours. Not too straight, not too curved. Did you ever consider going into the film business?"

The look on Sabrina's face told Amy as much as she needed to know about Alan Francis; more even than the diamond stud in his left ear.

"It could only have been you, Mr Blabbermouth, who told the press . . . about me, and about Josef's precious case."

"Not officially. It was just a drink in a pub."

"And your voice was wired up to every shitty newspaper in Britain!"

"It's a great story." Alan indicates his crew. "Without the publicity we'd not have got the funds to cover the presentation ceremony or make this film."

Amy's thoughts switch to JP. He's been in the thick of

things lately, and now with nothing to look forward to but the trip to more bad publicity and hate mail.

"We'll send you a postcard, JP." She gives him a kiss on the cheek. It is better than nothing.

First flight. A little scared. Should I ask Father Havran to say a prayer? I guess he's too ill to think about God at this moment. Fingers crossed that God's thinking about him.

She spares a thought for her auntie: I hope you'd approve of what I'm spending your lovely nest-egg on.

Father Havran is so ill he cannot eat his lunch. Josef eats his sweet; Amy his cheese. Alan is at the back of the plane, among the smokers. He waves once or twice. Amy ignores him.

Josef is pointing at an article on Prague in the glossy flight magazine. "See, Amy, Charles Bridge! And look, Wenceslas Square." He grins. "No tanks!"

And no sign of the man shaking his fist at the invaders; or the little boy on his shoulder, wearing the Basque cap and waving a placard. "True, instead there's a whopping great advert for soft drinks."

From Josef, a neat, philosophical shrug:

> Where the Rusky tank
> Draw a blank
> Coca-Cola score a goala!

Alan Francis warms to the Josef Sabata story the moment he sees the reception party of Very Important Persons at Prague's Ruzesyne airport. It is led by the Minister of Culture himself. There is also a large crowd of well-wishers eagerly applauding THE LOST JEWEL FOUND as one placard expresses it.

"Chaps," Alan announces to his crew, "I'm offering a free pub lunch minus drinks to the one who comes up with a jaunty and attention-grabbing title for this little number. And I'll not accept *Potty Poet Pulverises Prague*."

A couple of early suggestions are drowned out by the brass band—thirty of them. Alan giggles at the sight of their fancy uniforms. "After the drab old commies," he says, "comic opera!"

Czech TV isn't happy at Alan's bunch insisting on getting right in front of the action.

"BBC!" Alan has boomed, as though the very mention of the most famous broadcasting company in the world would have everybody falling over themselves to make way for him.

Father Havran translates the questions Czech journalists address to Amy: how did you meet Josef? What was he like then? What does it feel like to have breathed life back into a great poet?

"I just talked to him . . . When nobody else had the time . . . Read him *The Good Soldier Sveyk*."

What was the asylum like, Amy? Did they lock all the rooms? Were there padded cells? Was there solitary confinement? Did the authorities put people in there because they had been in trouble with the police?

Amy amuses her audience by asking, in turn, "Whose country are you talking about, mine or yours?"

Josef earns a few smiles with a few words: "It is my happiest day . . ." He is looking quite handsome, full-faced now, hair a silvery grey, eyes quick but kindly. "Since Ipswich won the cup!"

Behind the crowd of officials a young man watches the laughter but does not join in. He raises a small 35 millimetre camera which creates a very modest flash compared to those of the pressmen gathered round.

When the assembly prepares to depart for the city in official limousines, the young man stands by the entrance. He gets a good side-on picture of Josef and Amy together, she half a head taller.

Having watched the cars out of sight, he replaces the camera in the pocket of his grey mac. For several seconds he stares down at the ground, a hand across his eyes. Then, with a faintly discernible limp, he crosses the airport car park and unlocks his bicycle.

Josef and Amy are in Wenceslas Square with Alan and the film crew. Amy says, "I know I've only Clacton to compare it with, but I reckon Prague's the most beautiful city on earth."

A grin from Josef, and a nod. He puts his hand through her arm. "It is now!"

"Pure magic," admits Alan. "Those salmon-pink roofs will look a dream on film, contrasted with the green domes."

Wenceslas Square is more a vast sloping boulevard than a square. Josef has been stacked in front of everything that looks picturesque. When Amy had argued that Josef should be left to rest, Alan had replied, "We've got to grab these photo-opportunities while the light's so wonderful."

"Dr Parrish's orders—"

"Bugger Dr Parrish. Joe is enjoying himself. We're not asking him to make any speeches. In fact all he needs to do is smile and look poetic." He turns to his assistant. "Now, what's next, Sab?"

Sabrina reads out Alan's production jottings: "Next, Josef should be gazing with poetic gravity at the tribute to the . . . and you've written, 'student hero'."

"It'll be inscribed somewhere—"

"In Czech, though."

With impatience and growing exasperation, Amy snaps, "Jan Palach!"

Sabrina isn't happy: "You want my job?"

Alan ignores his assistant. "Remind me, Amy, as you seem so well informed."

"In protest at the Russians invading his country in '68, Jan Palach poured petrol over himself and set himself alight."

"But did Palach's sacrifice achieve anything?"

"Maybe it was a better thing to do than hide yourself away in a mental home for twenty years," observes Sabrina.

Josef has left them. His back is turned as he stoops over the flowers placed round the memorial to Palach and to all those who suffered under thirty years of tyranny.

Amy joins him, slips her arm through his. "And once upon a time, Josef, there was a father and his son. Round about here, I guess. Shaking fists at the tanks."

She does not expect an answer. He presses his hand over hers, smiles; he is so far away now. He murmurs, "Swimmers in the snow."

Amy notes the words, yet for the moment they don't make any sense.

"One of your poems, Josef?"

A nod. "Long, long ago."

"Are things any different now?"

A shake of the head.

Alan is saying to Sabrina, "Correct me if I'm wrong, but wasn't it the Poles who fought their corner during the Second World War while the Czechs threw in the towel without a fight?"

Amy finds herself defending the Czech nation. "Listen, Alan, I don't know what sort of film you've got in mind, but if you plan a demolition job, count us out."

"Am I right about that, though—the Czechs surrendered to Hitler without forcing him to break wind?"

"They'd no option, not after Britain and France stood back and let the Germans grab a chunk of Czechoslovakia bigger than Scotland."

Sabrina tries to defend her boss. "The Sudetenland was German—"

"German-speaking. It was as much a part of Czechoslovakia as England is of Britain."

"How come a teenager knows all this about a faraway country that's not even in the Common Market?"

"Because I care, that's why."

"They ought to offer you a job, Amy, in the new Ministry of Propaganda. Christ, woman, are you forgetting the basic facts? This Palach guy burnt himself for a cause and it took twenty years for the rest of them to light a candle.

"What's more, this whole damned nation must be full of collaborators after thirty years of Communism."

Amy turns away, stares at the flowers; bouquets of them, vases of them. "You'd know something about that, wouldn't you, Alan?"

"About what?"

"Collaboration . . . Isn't that what you journalists specialize in?"

"What the hell are you talking about?"

"Listen, where were you and your mates in the press when somebody was needed to protest about the death of my friend Spen? When boneheads worse than the worst Communists terrorize every neighbourhood from London to Glasgow, when families live in terror of firebombs coming through their front windows. Tell me, where're you lot when that happens?

"Complicity! That was my new word for the day before yesterday. It means keeping your mouth shut when you should be shouting from the rooftops. Your silence means more Nazis."

Amy points across the square towards a balcony beneath a huge M for Melantrich sign and the title of the newspaper *Svobodne Slovo*.

"Vaclav Havel spoke from that balcony, at the risk of another stint in jail. He challenged the high and mighty, while you lot crawl all over them. The last election at home— do you remember the lies every morning for breakfast?

"You make me sick. *You're* the poodles, you media people, so don't give me that rubbish about fighting your corner."

Amy Douglas' Wenceslas Square Speech is almost at an end. "As for Jan Palach, his sacrifice was repeated a million ways, every day. And when Havel spoke, thousands came. They showed two fingers to hundreds of cops who blocked their way.

"Two fingers to the truncheons and water cannon. Tell me, Alan, what would a supine nation like the Brits do in such a situation?"

Alan Francis just beams. "Supine? Have you swallowed a dictionary, darling?"

"If you want to know, 'supine' means lying on the back."

Alan Francis answers with his own word-of-the-day. "Like—inert!" He turns to his cameraman. "What did I tell you, Ed? This girl's a natural. A lioness of words! Did you get all that on tape, Jamie?"

"You bet!"

Dreamily, Josef is emerging from his own silence. "Marta sang."

Eddie's camera and Jamie's microphone close in on Josef who till now has refused to open his eyes when the camera faces him, or his mouth when the mike is switched on.

"Marta, Josef?"

"Marta sang. Oh yes!"

Sabrina checks her notes. "Marta Kubisova. She was banned from singing."

"Good," decides Alan. "We'll have her voice-over . . . Ever meet the lady, Josef?"

Josef speaks as from a cocoon of the past. "Marta sang. On the night of invasion, she sang a new song. On TV . . . Behind her, I remember, a picture of the Castle. Prayer for Marta—yes. They called it that."

"Do you remember the words, Joe? Could you recite them into camera? In English, then we'll voice-over her song in Czech. Okay?"

"It is a long time."

Amy waits. The song is in her head, for Josef has taught her the words. Josef glances at her, as if for confirmation. "Yes, Josef. It would be nice."

Sabrina breaks into the pause which follows. "It says here in my notes that Marta never sang again. They gave her a job as a machine-minder, making cardboard boxes."

"Okay, we'll do a take. Wait, Joe, for my signal. Sing away!"

Josef hesitates, grins, shrugs. The filming stops.

Amy offers a prompt: *"May over this our state . . ."*

Josef needs no further help. "Dobra—okay!"

> *May over this our state*
> *Lasting peace hold sway*
> *Oppression fear and hate*
> *Let them all pass away*
> *Pass away.*

Alan laughs as he signals Eddie to put the camera on hold. "And they made her fill cardboard boxes for that?"

Amy looks at Alan. "You understand nothing, do you, Alan? Absolutely nothing!"

Alan is brash. He refuses to be reached. "Me, I just make damn good movies—so count your blessings!"

Chapter Seven

Peace at last: and magic. It is nearly midnight in Prague. "We've made it, Josef!" Only just, but we've made it. Amy has suggested to him, "If you'd prefer to be alone . . ."

No, she is to stay with him. But permit him his own space. Anyhow, it's time to start up my own dreams. This is Charles Bridge with all the statues—thirty-one of them, says the guidebook—and two mighty towers at each end. Above everything looms the castle, the Hradcany, the 'c' pronounced like 'ch'. Beside it, all spires and pinnacles, is the cathedral of St Vitus, majestic against the stars.

Josef is staring up river. The lights dance on the water.

They are in a crowd: all Prague seems to want to watch the moonlight in the Vltava, the river which winds through the city.

"Dobra—you okay?"

Dobra. "Dekuju—thank you!"

She can't miss noticing the tears in his eyes.

There are still musicians serenading the frosty air; a couple of blind singers; a puppeteer escorting a fairy princess in a waltz, music provided by a tape recorder.

At the end of the bridge leading to the Old Town there is the sound of a hammer on metal and the flash of red coals. Two young men take it in turns to be blacksmith; what are they making?—who can tell, there is too much of a crowd.

Josef crosses to peer down river now. He points at one particular statue resplendent against the moon. "St John of Nepomuk."

"Is he the oldest?"

A nod. "Martyr. They tie his legs and arms, chuck him from the bridge."

"Don't tell me—for speaking out?"

A shake of the head. "For being on the wrong side."

Old cynic.

Amy has twice asked him if he has had enough for one day, but Josef's feet seem to have taken root on the bridge. I don't blame him. It's so beautiful. For me at this moment this is the most magical spot in the world.

Then why this tear, Amy Douglas? His wasted years, perhaps; and mine.

It's been a relief to get rid of Alan and the film crew. Nothing seems to mean a damn to those guys unless it's going to look good on film. "Stand in the Old Square, Joe—feed the pigeons and muse on the stories they could tell, about arrests in the night . . . Gaze at Jan Hus's statue, Joe, and think history while the hero of the Czechs whispers, voice-over, 'Truth Will Prevail'.

"Great quote—pity Hus got burnt at the stake for saying it . . . Now stare up at the fabulous old clock, Joe. See the skeleton—coming to fetch all of us sooner or later. Dwell on destiny, Joe!

"Okay, forget the clock. Now try one of the puppets." He grabbed one a metre in height from a nearby stall. "Permesso?" he asked in Italian. "Right, Joe. Think of invisible strings of power . . . manipulating the Czech nation from the Kremlin."

And all the while Josef meekly did what he was told, as if he was a prisoner grateful to escape a beating.

"And tomorrow, Joe, we want you to be wandering among the gravestones in the Jewish Cemetery, pondering on the meaning of Life, Death and the Everlasting."

Silly to ask, but Amy did: "What's the point of that, Alan, wandering in the cemetery?"

"Well, for a start, Joe is Jewish, right? He's searching for his roots again after all this time away. For his ancestors."

"But none of Josef's relatives was buried here in Prague. He's a Slovak, from near Bratislava."

"The great British public isn't interested in Czechs and Slovaks. Nobody is. Anyway, the Jewish Cemetery is a must. Without a visit, no tour of Prague is complete. It says so in the guidebook."

"And it makes great pictures, even if what you're telling the audience is a load of crap."

"Hey, Amy—give us a break. We're storytellers. Joe knows that. President Havel knows that. It's stories that make the world go round."

So that's for tomorrow; and then the next day is the ceremony up at the Castle.

A tissue for Josef to blow his nose. "Thinking of the old days, Josef?"

"Oh no. Bad times, the old times."

"Then why the tears? Is it because tonight's so beautiful?"

A shrug. "My country, I think."

"Seems wonderful to me—freedom at last. Independence."

"But do you not feel it?"

"Feel? What should I feel?"

"Beneath the surface. How do you say in English . . . seething?"

Ah, what was it Josef once said back at High Lawns? Good

78

poets can see through brick walls; they shake with the earth-quake before it happens.

"No more seething than Britain, I'd say."

"Britain is asleep."

"Okay, but here everything's so relaxed now, so friendly. All the music. People going to restaurants. Not looking over their shoulders in fear any more. No electronic bugs sello-taped under the table. All gone."

Amy is surprised. None of this seems to make Josef happy. He shakes his head. "But my people—the Czechs, the Slo-vaks . . . seething."

"So what are you going to do about it now you're back, Josef?"

"I can do nothing."

"You said poems can move mountains. That they're like bombs which can overthrow governments."

"Not here, not any longer . . . You see, how can a poem be a bomb when poets become presidents?"

There is still a crowd on the bridge, though the blacksmiths have wheeled off their armoury. Lovers kiss beneath the statues. The sight of them momentarily saddens Amy. Here you are, under moon and stars, with a crumbly old poet; talking politics. I even fancy the chap over there with the limp, though his face is lost in shadow.

I think he's been eyeing me up.

Josef is saying, "I am sad because there is no point in being a poet, not any longer."

"You don't always have to be a rebel, silly. There are other reasons why people love poetry."

"Here, no. You must understand that, Milacku. The old regime, the Communists, they put us in jail. Then we had something to fight against. Our words, they meant some-thing. Because when we uttered them, people took notice.

Our words earned us a beating, a prison sentence. The better our poems, the worse our punishment.

"When they deprived us of rations, of light, of exercise, of letters from home, we knew our poems were true ones."

"Did you get letters from home, Josef?"

A shake of the head: his past remains the mystery it always was.

"And now, what are you saying—that your poems don't mean anything any more?"

"Now, for my poems, they give me a medal. They greet the poet with a military band. I am welcomed in marble halls. Soon Josef Sabata will write jingles for television:"

> *I'd rather suffer epilepsy*
> *Than do without my Pepsi;*
> *I'd rather end up broke*
> *Than do without my Coke.*

"Nobody's asking you to sell your soul."

"Look at the world—they will!"

Amy remembers Sylvia Benson's strict instructions for Josef: "Bed early and don't allow him to dwell on things." It's time to be matron. "Come on, Josef, you must be whacked. It's still ten minutes to the hotel."

A fierce stamp of the foot. "Whacked? Me, I do nothing but stand and look like zombie feeding damn pigeons. No. I want to go on a tram!"

"Now?"

"Best at night, the trams in Prague."

"But where to?"

"As you say in English, there and back . . . How does it go?"

"There and back to see how far it is."

Josef begins to trot. "Come on—we try Number 17. It passes along the river."

The next bridge up river spans an island, and at the corner of the street opposite is a café—the Slavia—which Josef promises to take Amy to. "In those days, if you want to send message to secret police, you book table—that overlook river. And just talk. Fun, really!"

They have been issued sheets of tickets for the tram, the bus or the underground. You rip off a ticket and stick it into a metal hole-punch as you climb aboard. This tram's not like the majority, red and cream; it's painted blue with a giant picture of a yellow camel down one side.

"Yanky fags!" says Josef disapprovingly. Camels aren't his favourite. On board, a few glazed and tired faces; and a girl who prefers to stand despite there being empty seats.

Josef points. He remembers everything. "Narodni—the Opera House."

Up before five this morning, Amy is tired out, but Josef seems to be on a high. Another stop; a queue—but they don't queue in Prague. A crowd. She hardly notices until there is a fist banging on the window.

Eyes wide now: boneheads out on the town. Ignore them. If you let them catch your eye, you provoke them. Just tell yourself—they're dogshit, littering every pavement in every city on earth; so why not here?

Yet Amy is forced to take notice when she realizes it's Josef not she who's the centre of the youths' attention. She hears the words, "Juden! Juden!"

Suddenly I know we're in a fix. There are ten or eleven of them, some with heads shaved, jangling with badges; one with a swastika tattooed on his forehead. Just how our own bootboys used to dress till they got smart and began to wear suits and ties.

Amy hears the girl standing behind her say something as the youths stampede on board the tram.

Spen, where are you when I need you?

The youths are pulling Josef from his seat, lifting him up almost to the roof of the tram. "No Jews!"

"Jews off!"

That much Amy understands. She is up. They are planning to dump Josef off the tram. "What the bloody hell! Get the hell off him!"

They turn on Amy, thrust her back over the seat. She strikes out but only encounters leatherlook and medals.

Yet there's help: the girl is shouting in Czech. For her pains she is flung against the opposite window, almost into a passenger's lap.

Josef is not going to stand for this nonsense either. He levers himself up, grasps a hanging strap with one hand and the nose of an assailant with the other.

A knee up into his ribs doubles him over. He slides behind the seat.

"No Jews!"

"Leave him alone!" Amy is poked hard in the face. She lashes out but her arm is trapped. She receives a blow in the chest.

This action silences the other passengers who were beginning to speak up in Amy's defence.

The Bonehead SS are yanking Josef out, kneeing him in the back, flicking his head. Amy's nose is gushing.

Like old times.

Her injury doesn't prevent her bringing one of them down, over the back of a seat and whamming him in the balls with her forearm. He howls in agony.

Sometimes war can be wonderful.

Amy is going to be eternally grateful to her new comrade-in-arms who calls out in English, "Shout!—as loud as you can."

The tram driver has brought his vehicle to a halt. He too is up, bellowing at the youths—but they will have their way.

"No Jews on Czech trams!"

"No Slovaks!"

"No gypos!"

Amy is roaring stuff in English. History is doing an action replay, because this is Spen and me all over again. Who was it said, 'If you live long enough you meet yourself coming back'? Well I'm seeing killers' eyes and they're fixed on me; and my new pal, who's kicking out at every prick in sight.

What turns things around is the driver's action. He has produced a spanner the size of a riot baton. It's his tram, he seems to be yelling, and nobody puts paying passengers off his tram.

The skins have had their joke. Josef is on the ground between the seats. They've kicked him in the chest and Amy thinks she hears his ribs crack.

They Zieg Heil, and the faces are the faces Amy has seen at home. Yet the British bones, they're just ignorant sods. Thick as pigshit. These, though, these are worse because their dads and their grandads must have known the Nazis at first hand.

Remember what the guidebook said? During the holocaust, over 77,000 Czech Jews were exterminated by the Nazis.

The tram driver's spanner doesn't have to shout like the two women have had to do. It whispers in the air and the boneheads descend from Tram 17 and whoop the night. Any more Jews? Any gypos?

"Are you okay?" the girl asks Amy.

"Thanks, not really." Both of us, lifting Josef on to one of the seats.

"I'm Vera. I am so sorry . . ."

"I'm Amy. You were so good to—"

"He will need treatment." The driver is about twenty; nice looking. His long hair is bundled behind his head with double elastic. Amy realizes he too is speaking English. She is bleeding all over the place. He takes her arm. There is dark hair on the back of his hands. "And so will you."

A smile from Vera. "This is my brother Jiri." Yes, the resemblance is clear, though Vera's hair is curly and cut short.

Jiri races down the tram, returns with a toilet roll. Amy says "Thanks" and bungs a wad under her nose. He says, "Great!" and Amy decides this means, "'You were great'".

One eye is about to swell up.

Josef is nursing his ribs, but there is no sign of defeat in him. He has no breath, but he is demanding a fag. Jiri has meanwhile jumped off the tram. He is in the middle of the road, flagging down a taxi.

He returns within a minute. "Sorry, but I have a schedule to keep." He helps his sister and Amy ease Josef along the tram and down the steps.

Josef is rubbing his ribs, coughing, suddenly looking terribly frail.

Bastards! Things were going so well.

Jiri apologizes first on behalf of his tram—whose honour seems to have been damaged more seriously than if he'd collided with a Number 24; then on behalf of the people of Prague, the Czech people and finally the Czechoslovak nation.

"I am disgusted and ashamed." He grunts, shakes his fist in the direction of the vanished youths. "Under the Communists, that did not happen."

His sister takes issue. "No, they just beat up students instead."

"You *expect* the authorities to beat people up. It's what they're paid for in the end. But when the young pick on the old, what then?"

"You got freedom!"

Jiri and Vera help the wounded to the awaiting taxi. "Go with them, Vera. They'll need a translator."

As soon as Josef realizes he is hospital-bound, he protests that he is all right. There is terror in his voice:

"No hospital!"

"Just to be on the safe side, Josef." I remember I also need looking at. There's blood all over my coat. My eye's throbbing too. It'll be blue-black in the morning.

I'm thinking, Alan and his film crew won't be pleased: bad for continuity; Josef bent over with a broken rib, me with a face that needs a bag over it.

"It's not far," says Vera. I let her take my hand. It's a wonderful comfort. "Where're you staying?"

I tell her and comment on how good her English is.

"I am a tourist guide."

"Not a student?"

"A student *and* a tourist guide."

"And Jiri?" I try not to seem too interested.

"He's a student too, an art student. But these are tough days."

"This is Josef, what's left of him. Your boneheads beat up one of Czechoslovakia's greatest poets, though to them I suppose that would be a cause for celebration."

"Josef Sabata?"

Well here's a bonus. "You've read about him?"

"He is in all the papers."

Amy cannot make out whether Vera considers this good news, for her companion's gaze falls away and there is an awkward silence. "I have also read his poetry. From long ago."

"It's wonderful, isn't it?"

Vera's is a strangely guarded reply; as if she fears she is being secretly tape-recorded, and thus has to choose her words carefully. "Oh yes. My father thought him a great poet."

Amy decides Vera is a little bit in awe of her friend. "Hear that, Josef? Somebody's actually read your poetry."

Josef is sinking into an old mood. He is shaking, partly with shock, partly in fury. "Then she should be locked up!"

Chapter Eight

When Amy learns that Vera has missed her last metro and thus her last bus home, she says, "You can stay in my room at the hotel. I'll wait with Josef."

The hospital doctor has decided to keep the old man in over night for observation. He has also staunched Amy's bleeding nose and provided a cool pad for her swelling eye.

"I'm in no hurry," replies Vera. The waiting room is empty except for them. Vera puts up her legs, makes herself comfortable. "The last time I was in a place like this was for my dad. The news wasn't so good."

"Was he beaten up?"

"Not on that occasion." Plainly Vera does not wish to talk about it. Amy guesses she must be near twenty. She looks a fighter—stocky, quick of movement, yet with gentle, almost grey eyes that seem to smile at you even when her face is perfectly straight.

Her hair is an unruly mass of curls which every now and then Vera tries to comb out with her fingers as if she'd always dreamed of having straight hair.

"Should we report it all to the police?" asks Amy.

Hand among curls again, anxiously pulling them over her ear as if to test whether she has heard aright. "Police?"

Don't say this girl's in trouble with the cops too.

"Well that's what they're there for, to protect the community."

"Oh yes. Of course. In your country I suppose that's what happens."

Amy won't go that far. "Sure, if you're white, washed and have some place to live."

Vera is surprised; for her, Britain has often seemed the land over the rainbow. She shrugs. "Here in Czechoslovakia, until a little time ago, if you report anything to the police, well, they start asking *you* the questions."

"But things are different now . . . Aren't they?"

Vera remembers her duty as a tourist guide is to be diplomatic about the Velvet Revolution. "Oh yes, a lot of things are different. Anyway, you are right. We must report the attack on your . . ." She breaks off.

"Adopted grandad. I'm his nurse, really. Also, his swimming instructor." A smile. "And his bodyguard!"

Some bodyguard. Josef is asleep now, but in the moments before he dozed off, he seemed to have difficulty recognizing Amy. "No thank you," he had said in English when she leant over the bed.

"Josef, it's me, Amy. They've not broken your ribs. Just severely bruised them. Does it hurt bad?"

A tiny, wry smile. He remembers his young friend and bodyguard: "Does it hurt *badly*, Milacku—where did you learn your English?"

He's going to be okay.

Even so, Amy decides to take another look at Josef before they leave the hospital. On her return to the waiting room, she gets a surprise. Vera's brother Jiri has arrived. He decides on a formal greeting and shakes Amy's hand.

"You were very brave." Same bright eyes as Vera, though he seems to Amy to be more stressed; wound up, even.

He has called to take Vera home. "Max has his car—he can drop us at the bottom of Davidkova."

Vera says no. "I'll stay with Amy tonight. Just in case."

Amy feels Jiri's eyes on her, looking her over with a special interest.

"I wish to apologize for my fellow countrymen," he says in excellent English.

"And I wish to thank you on behalf of your fellow countryman, Josef Sabata."

A glance from brother to sister; Vera nods.

"Sabata?" Jiri reacts without pleasure.

"And you—what is your . . . ?"

"Bodyguard."

Things are tense. Amy feels the atmosphere but cannot begin to understand such a reaction.

She guesses Vera is coming to her rescue when her new friend adds, "And swimming instructor."

"You swim?"

How nervy this guy is; another word and he'll snap. "A little."

Jiri is recalling what he has read in the papers of the Josef Sabata story. "You are the girl who discovered our hero?"

Vera intrudes. "Won't Max be getting impatient, Jiri?"

"I swim too. Tomorrow—would you like to swim? Early?"

"How early's early?"

"Six-thirty?" There is a challenge in his look, but also a glimmer of doubt. This Jiri is not as confident in himself as he would like to appear.

But Amy Douglas needs her swim. "Six-thirty."

"I am Jiri—what is your name, please?"

"Amy."

"Six-thirty then, Amy."

*   *   *

89

On the way back to the hotel, Amy and Vera pass through the Old Town square. Each of the twin towers of the Tyn Church sprouts a spire; each spire sprouts four pinnacles; each pinnacle sprouts a golden orb and each orb seems to have a shred of moonlight attached to it.

"It's hard to picture tanks in this fairy land," says Amy, "crashing over these wonderful cobbles."

"And water cannon. They shoot those at us when we march to Wenceslas Square in 1989. That day we called *The Masakyr*. I have bruises for weeks afterwards."

"And Jiri, did he protest too?"

"He was—how do you say?—a true fish in water. So brave! But reckless. Got a broken head." A sigh. "It was his day of glory."

"And now?"

"Nothing is the same. No more heroes—just rising prices."

"You said he was an artist."

"Once upon a time. All he ever did lately is paint a tank."

"The Pink Tank?"

"You have heard of it?"

"It was in our papers. A Russian tank in one of the city squares. One day it was boring old camouflage, the next it was pink all over!"

Amy forgets Jiri's bad mood; if you paint a tank pink you're bound to be one of the Good Guys.

Vera too cannot conceal her pride. "Yes, with his pals. They have postcards of it now . . . But then Jiri immediately regret it, for he says—the world laughs at the Czechs as well as the tank."

Globes of white light float ahead of them down the narrow alleys. Bars are still open. "Along there, Amy, is the Theatre on the Balustrade, where they performed Havel's plays. Until they were banned.

"And my father, he once give lecture there—on the dangers of pollution in our country . . . The police stop him halfway through, and arrest a hundred people."

Sooner or later, Amy perceives, Vera steers the conversation round to her father; yet it makes her unhappy, brings her to a full stop.

"What happened to your dad, Vera? Mine died in a car crash."

Vera straightens her curls, smiles and says the oddest thing. "You would make a first-class interrogator, Amy."

They are back by the river again.

"And my mother," Amy persists, "she died in the same accident. Since then I've always taken an interest in other people's parents."

Vera seeks refuge in her role as tourist guide. She is not used to talk like this. "See to the left of the Castle? That's Petrin Hill. Lovely walks up there. At the top of the Petrin is located a viewing tower modelled on the Eiffel Tower, built in 1891.

"It stands sixty metres in height and offers to the visitor Prague's most beautiful panorama. I would take you there but it is closed for the winter."

It's late, Amy is tired, all of her face is hurting and she doesn't approve of word-fencing. She asks, impatiently, "Are we or aren't we going to be friends, Vera?"

Vera stops, pulls tenaciously at her curls. "Well you must first understand us, the Czech people. For years and years, we say nothing. We tell nothing. We trust no one, for fear they betray us. Not even our family, our friends. We keep our secrets—always.

"Big Brother was everywhere. Can you understand that? So it is difficult, this new freedom . . . Cripples—is that right? Jiri says we are cripples. Our feelings, we lock away.

Tight, so tight that, well, sometimes . . . Well never mind."

Amy makes a guess. "Sometimes you can't trust even your brother?"

It touches the mark. "Or yourself.

"And that is horrible—horrible! Perhaps once trust is gone, perhaps it is dead for ever." Vera looks at Amy as if, coming from another culture in a faraway country, she might have brought a comforting answer.

Amy dumps words. She offers, and Vera welcomes, a hug. It is a wonderful feeling; and almost compensates for the pain in Amy's eye, swollen as a pumpkin.

A shock awaits them back at the hotel. Josef's room has been ransacked. The bed has been stripped, chairs upturned. The wardrobe doors are wide open and Josef's new suit and other clothes scattered on to the floor. Drawers from the dressing table have been removed and emptied.

Amy suddenly dives out of the room in the middle of Vera saying, "At the least, they did not pinch his silver pencil." Into the corridor, thick-carpeted, to her own room, wrenching at the key.

"Oh come on!"

The room is exactly as Amy had left it. And exactly where Amy had left it, on the bed, complete with plastic name tag and the address of High Lawns, is Josef's precious case.

Pain-in-the-ass Pandora.

She picks it up, checks whether it has been tampered with.

Vera is behind her. "Not thieves, I think."

"How can you tell?"

Vera holds up the silver propelling pencil. "Your friend brings documents, does he not?"

Amy sits on the bed, pulling Pandora across her knees.

92

"Who knows? Josef won't say. He just laughs. Blame the press, they're suckers for secrets."

"They say your friend possesses names."

"Look, Josef's got a name. He used to be Sir Stubborn or Josef Kastov—now he's somebody!"

"And possibly dangerous."

Do I really like these Czechs? They're full up to their eyeballs in suspicion. "Kafka!" Amy says, staring at the dull brown leather of Josef's mysterious case. "The whole thing. Somebody round here is on trial. I'm not sure who. And I'm damned if I know why."

She glances up at Vera. "Well?"

"We should tidy up Josef's room." Vera kisses her on the cheek. "And then a strong coffee—okay?"

A bit of warmth at last. Amy tries out her Czech: "Dobra!" She taps Pandora. "But first we put this little timebomb in the hotel safe."

Vera remains troubled. "It would probably be more wise to throw it into the Vltava."

Amy agrees. "Unfortunately that would be as bad for Josef as throwing *him* into the Vltava." She sighs. "So it's not been such a good night for fairy tales after all."

Vera has taken a bottle of Bechers from the fridge. She pours two full glasses, raises her own. "Welcome to Prague!"

The barrier that existed between the two women appears to have melted away. Vera says, "Tomorrow I am not free. I have lectures to go to. But Jiri, he takes a tour—Americans. Of the Castle, Golden Lane and the Strahov Monastery.

"He is a good guide. Why not join him? No charge, of course."

The Strahov is where Josef's literary works are to be housed, in the Museum of Literature. "I'd love to. So long as it's okay with Josef."

Amy drinks. Her thoughts turn to Jiri. There's an attraction, pretty sure about that. At least on my side. She asks, "Did your brother mean it about swimming so early?"

Vera tops up Amy's glass. "Well, I have never known Jiri make such a crazy invitation before. So I think the answer must be yes."

"And if he asks for a race?"

"Be sure to beat him!"

The next morning the telephone rings from hotel reception at exactly six-thirty. Jiri's first words to Amy are just what Vera would probably have predicted of him. "Don't say you've forgotten?" It's as if he really wants to be disappointed in people.

"Give me five minutes." Amy scrambles into her clothes, grabs a towel and her costume and tucks her goggles into her pocket. "Vera?"

Dead to the world.

Jiri has borrowed his friend Max's car. "Trabant!" he announces with as much pride as might the owner of a new BMW. "It is a collector's item now. We visited the factory in East Germany. Swapped it for Max's viola."

Collector's item? Poison wagon. The interior is full of blue smoke. "It is difficult on frosty mornings."

Amy decides against telling Jiri about last night's break-in. After all, this is the Land of Suspicion according to Vera; and who knows, Jiri might have been the burglar.

"How's the eye?"

"I can see through it."

"I reported the incident to my boss. He asked if there was any damage to the tram. I said, 'No, the only damage was to the good name of the Czech people'."

"And what did he say?"

" 'Well that's all right, then'!"

The pool is magnificent; Olympic size, and almost empty.

"When I swim," confides Jiri, "the world becomes a better place."

He gazes at Amy with approval as she stands at the poolside. She considers him in good shape too.

"Race, Amy?"

I was right. It's to be the old war of the sexes. "I'll need to warm up a bit."

"Of course. Four lengths?"

Okay, play it coy: don't men expect it? "I'm not sure I can manage that at this time of morning."

"Take your time then." Jiri goes for a bellysmack dive. He does the crawl, not badly but not well either. She smiles, for he can't keep straight, angling across the pool, and reminding her of mornings back home and a swimmer they called Diagonal Donald.

She slips into the water. Not snow this; but the eternal green of spring, clear down to the white tiles and the red stripe which denotes the deep end.

Jiri finishes his four lengths as Amy completes her third, doing a sedate breaststroke. He waits for her, puffing.

They pause, shoulders almost touching. "You have a boyfriend, Amy?"

He doesn't waste time. "You have a girlfriend, Jiri?" He shakes his head, but not convincingly. "That's strange, because Vera says you have scores of them."

"Vera is my worst enemy."

"You say that almost as if you meant it."

He is embarrassed. "What about that race?"

Amy shrugs, diffident, taps her chest as if to indicate she might not have the breath for it.

"Don't worry. I will give you a start."

Do men ever cease to be boys? "How much of a start?"

"Half a length?"

"Four lengths, then?"

Jiri had not counted on another four. He hesitates.

"Or would you prefer six?"

He laughs: English women, they've got this streak of arrogance. "Four will be sufficient."

"Loser pays for breakfast, right?"

"Right." English women are also loaded with cash.

Away: an easy breaststroke once more, not even ducking her head beneath the water. At the half-length point Amy hears Jiri give a competitive yell and then call out, "To a great breakfast!"

Show-off. He has swum a third of a length under water; expects to rise to the surface right on her tail. Instead, he meets Amy coming back. It puzzles him. She must have speeded up.

Legs and arms flail to make up the loss. At the pool end he gives himself a savage push off. He wishes he had worn his own goggles because the lashing from his arms makes it impossible to see his adversary.

Jiri lifts his head from the water. His spirit soars. He is catching up. But for getting a mouthful and simultaneously forgetting to breathe, he would have goaded her with a triumphant "Czechs for ever!"

They are neck and neck. He knew it. She's put everything she's got into this race, but now her strength's spent. She's blown it. One thing's for certain in this life, the tortoise never beats the hare.

Victory is a length away. Jiri does not know exactly why at this moment but winning will be so sweet. Better even than the day of the pink tank.

Admittedly there is the little matter of him doing crawl and

Amy persisting with slow old breaststroke; but then after all, this is a freestyle race.

Who dares, wins!

Jiri is a stroke ahead. What he has not noticed, and what Amy will decline to tell him, is that she had waited for him in mid-pool. He flings himself out on the last glorious length.

In this life you've got to beat somebody; if you're a Czech, he reminds himself, that's particularly important. And he remembers his father telling him about the super Olympic victory of the Czech ice-hockey team over the Russians; how the nation celebrated!

Trust the Russians to come in with their tanks in revenge.

Something passes him. For a moment he thinks another swimmer has dived in from the side. Then he realizes there's about to be an Olympic-size upset.

Amy has reverted to crawl. Her style is rhythmic, seemingly effortless. In moments she is so far in front of him that he could not catch her up even by running along the poolside.

She is waiting for him at the shallow end. "Breakfast?"

He takes defeat well: another Czech characteristic. "How do you manage to be so fast?"

She leans towards him. This is their first touch. She flips back the hair from his eyes. "I practise by swimming in the snow."

Chapter Nine

Amy opts for her free breakfast at Josef's favourite café, the Slavia. It overlooks the Vltava, offers a view of the Castle and of the spot where, last night, she and Josef boarded Jiri's tram.

"Fate brought us together," believes Jiri.

Amy decides to take a break from being the arch cynic. "I think it did." *I'm not usually this attracted to a boy, not first off.*

Jiri is darker than his sister. Like her he is quick in his movements, jerky even. Like Vera he seems to be struggling all the time to rein in a troublesome impatience.

He is wearing a baggy marine blue suit and a dazzling orange T-shirt with the words *Have a Nice Stay* on the front. His long hair is in a pony-tail. His left toe is sticking out of a pair of Polish-made sneakers.

One of the Americans on Jiri's guided tour will shortly comment, "Son, you look like you stepped right out of the Sixties." At which Jiri will reply, with a grin, "We never had any Sixties in Czechoslovakia. They were banned."

"Amy, I have a confession to make."

"You thought you were going to win our race so you left your money at home?"

"Not exactly. I just don't have enough to pay for us. Not till I get some tips from today's tour."

Amy passes money under the table. "Hey, they'll think I'm a male prostitute."

"I'm sure it would have been worth every penny."

At the hospital, Josef was grumpy but relishing his breakfast. "The doctor is going to keep you in till lunchtime. I'm to call for you at two on the dot."

Josef was in pain; lying down was hard, so was sitting up. What worried Amy most was Josef saying that he'd had a visit from Mr Dodds. "I told him, no more chess till he washes egg off his shirt. He went off to sulk."

"We're not at High Lawns, Josef. We're thirty-odd hours off you being awarded a medal by the President. So you've got to take care. Rest this morning, and I'll tell Alan—no filming at the cemetery. You're not up to it and it's too cold to be standing about."

"No. I wish to visit the cemetery. I promised."

"Okay, you can look beautiful among the gravestones for fifteen minutes only. Then we're taking it easy for the rest of the evening."

"I do not want to take it easy."

"Doctor's orders."

"I have not come to Prague to sip tea. I want Prague beer. My damaged ribs demand it. Gallons of it!"

Amy had phoned the hotel. She caught Vera on her way out. They agreed to meet on Charles Bridge at one o'clock. "If you see the film crew, Vera, please don't mention the hospital. Say Josef's sleeping in till the afternoon."

"Well, last night they drank the bar dry. I guess they'll be—"

"Comatose?"

"Comatose?"

"It's what my English teacher said we all were on Friday afternoons."

"Meaning?"

"They'll be in a stupor till midday."

Jiri's coachload of American tourists are middle-aged and elderly, yet full of high spirits. They are charmed by the young, good-looking Czech who does not seem to take history too seriously. The morning is crisp and bright. The city's spires and domes and gold-gleaming pinnacles revel in a cloudless sky.

"Ladies and gentlemen," announces Jiri at the first port-of-call, Castle courtyard, "a terrible thing happened to this great obelisk of marble when it was being transported here to the Castle of Hradcany—somebody with butter fingers went and dropped it, broke it clean in two."

Amy wonders, could it have been Sveyk?

"Well they've done a good job with the bits, Jiri," says a sixty-odd year old called Sidney.

"That is, if you do not look too closely, Sir. Just like our country. We are split from top to bottom, Czechs one side, Slovaks the other. Then there are Germans who want to be German again, Hungarians who want to be Hungarian and Rusyns who want to be Rusyns—it's all the rage! I doubt if we will survive till the summer."

"You know what we did when the Southern States tried to break away from the Union, Jiri?" asks Melvyn, a retired attorney from Philadelphia. "We put our foot down. Your Mister President must do the same!"

Jiri receives this advice with a smile. "I'll have a word with President Havel next time we meet."

In introducing Amy to his customers, Jiri has said, "This is Amy Douglas from Britain. She put her foot down and got

100

the black eye." He has described the scene on Tram 17. Amy becomes an instant heroine among the Americans.

"You sure got problems, Jiri," agrees Charlotte, a tall, skinny lady from Denver. "What with Commies and Nazis—"

"And gypsies," intrudes Arnold from St Louis. "Nobody here seems to like 'em."

Okay, Jiri, get yourself out of this one.

"My father used to say," replies the tour guide, "that people always hate those they have done wrong."

His comment is unexpected. He leaves it at that. "This way, ladies and gentlemen!" Jiri leads his customers to a terrace overlooking the city. "Praha!" he announces. "The word means 'threshold'."

Prague is veiled in a light-haze of palest blue. The outlines of spires and cupolas blur into each other. Towers stand protectively above shadowed streets and the focus of every sweep of the eye is the Vltava, silver-glinting beneath Charles Bridge.

"The city of *The Good Soldier Sveyk*, ladies and gentlemen, of Franz Kafka, of Smetana, Dvořák, Martinu and . . . of my father."

"What does he do, Jiri?"

"What did he do? He was a scientist and a philosopher."

"Stuck him in prison, did they?"

Jiri puts his finger to his nose. "I am afraid we guides are forbidden to give personal details."

Amy feels the magic of the city, but she also feels decidedly groggy. Perhaps she's caught Father Havran's flu; perhaps it is a reaction to last night—the attack on Josef—"No Jews!"; the attempted burglary, then all the talk about names.

Bloody names! And no doubt Jiri's thinking his dad might also be on the list.

She is not taking in the information that pours from Jiri so abundantly. This is the Schwarzenberg Palace, an exemplary work of Prague Renaissance; home of the Military History Museum.

"I didn't think you Czechs had any military history, Jiri," calls Abe from Nebraska.

Nothing throws Jiri. "For the first thousand years we Bohemians were very warlike. Then we got wise. We started eating garlic which we breathed over our enemies. And that sent them running."

"It didn't send the Jerries running, did it? Or the Ruskies?"

Jiri is not happy for the Nazis and the Russians to be linked in one breath. He smiles. "True, garlic had no power over sauerkraut . . . But please remember, it was the Russians who liberated the Czechs from the Nazi evil."

"Were you a Red, Jiri?" asks Enid from Albuquerque.

Jiri chooses to press on with his itinerary. "And over there, ladies and gentlemen, are the palace guard in their new-style uniforms. On the hour, they burst into song and stick roses down their rifle barrels."

Jiri earns welcome laughter.

"It does seem that much of our life here in Prague is straight from a costume comedy. But can you blame us? The past has been so dreary."

"How come, Jiri, the Commies preserved all these churches?" asks Dan from Wisconsin.

"Same reason the Nazis preserved the Jewish Museum. As monuments to the mistakes of the past."

So bitter; and this time nobody laughs, for there are Jews in the party.

A glance at Amy; a shrug—who knows?

And now a brisk descent to famous Golden Lane. "Here dwelt Franz Kafka, ladies and gentlemen, one of Czechoslovakia's most famous, and most misunderstood writers, between 1912 and 1914—in this tiny street of tiny houses. Look at the brilliant colours. Notice that the houses are so small they have foldaway stairs."

"Pokey," says Iris from Kansas. "No wonder Kafka got depressed."

"What went on here, Jiri?"

"This was the street of the alchemists. I predict that soon it will be auctioned off and shipped to the Metropolitan Museum in New York."

"Shame!" calls Orville from L.A. "California would be a much better place for it—if you throw in Charles Bridge as well!"

"And shame on you, Orville," reproves his wife, Millie. "You can't put a price on such things."

"On the contrary, Madam," replies Jiri. "These days in my country there is a price placed upon everything. Everything is up for auction. Only our people cannot pay the price . . . And now we shall spend a few moments in the Cathedral of St Vitus, where Kafka set a scene in his novel *The Trial*."

"What about *The Good Soldier Sveyk* you mentioned earlier?" asks Ned, a teacher from Vermont. "Didn't he haunt these streets?"

"Sveyk was a boozer. When he wasn't kidnapping and selling pet dogs, he was to be found in Prague's many pubs, especially in U Kalicha, The Chalice."

Amy is peckish. She wants to ask, "Isn't it coffee and cake time?" Instead, she learns how, in the Romanesque church of St George, the roof beams had been soaked in ox-blood; and for that reason they look as new today as they did hundreds of years ago.

Ox-blood. Could it cure black eyes?

At last a break from ancient monuments: coffee, just up a

cobbled street from the Strahov. "I promise this will be the highlight of your visit to Prague, ladies and gentlemen. The Strahov houses the Museum of Czechoslovak Literature, our proudest possession."

No cynicism now; instead, a glow of pure pride.

The Americans seem to sense there's something between their guide and the young lady with the blonde hair and the black eye, so the two of them are left with a table to themselves. "They think we're lovers," says Jiri. "How about it?"

"I never make love in the back of a Trabant."

The waiter interrupts, placing a pot of coffee and a plate of cakes between them—ordered by Jiri's customers. They glance round and cups are raised.

It could be the moment for anything. They are together. They are attracted to each other. They are close. But caution prompts Amy to shift the topic of conversation on to safer ground.

Trust—that's got to come first. At the moment, for Amy, Jiri is too much like a bottle of fizzy drink that's been shaken till the top is about to shoot off.

But is it harmless lemonade or petrol?

One minute he is down, the next, bright as a skyrocket; full of pessimism, full of hope; lashed by doubt then bouncing with confidence.

Which could mean he'll love me on his way up and hate me on his way down. Believe me, High Lawns has nothing on you, Jiri. Yet she is excited. This relationship is moving. Her mind advises her to pull back but her instinct is to take risks.

Don't let things settle—push on.

So Amy brings up the one topic she is sure will make her would-be lover sore—Josef Sabata and the honour he is to receive from his fatherland. "You know, it was a miracle Josef's poems ever reached Prague."

She describes how Father Havran drove from London in an old Cortina, the boot loaded with four plastic boxes packed with Josef's verses. "Somewhere between Leipzig and the Czech border he dozed off at the wheel and hit a tree. The boot of the Cortina burst open and Josef's poems flew all over the place like a blizzard.

"Father Raven is pretty sure he rescued everything, but it'll take the people at the Strahov ages to put it all in order."

"I'm sorry—what did you say?"

"Josef's work is to be catalogued in the Strahov." Amy speaks with undisguised pride. "His poems will be preserved for ever."

Jiri's reaction at this connecting of his revered Strahov and Josef Sabata is dramatic and indicates to Amy that she has pushed her luck too far.

The news stuns him. He almost smashes his coffee cup as he replaces it in the saucer. His fist closes. He would strike the table with it but his customers are watching.

He lays his hand palm down on the table. "In the Strahov, of all places?"

"Why not?"

This time Jiri fails to control his temper. He shouts, "Why not?" Then he remembers himself, grins at the Americans, some of whom have decided to go out and stand in the warm sun.

"Yes, Jiri, why not?"

"Because Sabata does not deserve it, that is why!"

"Because his poetry isn't good enough?"

"You would not understand."

"Because he stayed away from things so long?"

"I do not wish to talk about it."

"Or because your father didn't make it to the Strahov?"

If ever there was an idiot thing to say, Amy realizes instantly, this is it.

Jiri stands up. He does not speak, does not look at her. He is white.

How about that, Amy Douglas?—you're on the point of falling in love, when suddenly Old Dame Motormouth goes and blows everything to bits.

Congratulations!

Yet this mood, almost of submission, of admitting she has done something stupid and wrong, is swiftly flushed out by its opposite, a sense of injustice, even of righteousness: I've done nothing wrong and nor has Josef.

It's this bugger, all charm one minute, mean and resentful the next. You owe him nothing so don't put up with it. Bloody kid!

He has walked out of her space, leaving Betty from Montana to accompany Amy out into the street. Jiri is ahead of his band, striding towards the gates of the Strahov.

What's it with these Czechs? Not realizing she is rubbing salt into a wound, Betty says, "He's a handsome boy, isn't he?"

Amy is in two minds: which is it to be—leave now and admit you've been hurt, or spend the rest of the tour being snubbed and feeling terrible?

I'll do a bunk in my own good time, thank you. And no envious turd is going to stop me seeing where Josef's poems are to be displayed alongside the manuscripts of Kafka.

That's my contribution to history, Mrs A.

"Ladies and gentlemen, we are now entering the second oldest religious building in Prague." Jiri races his speech. He is all at once avoiding eye-contact with anyone and the zest has gone out of his voice. "It houses a library of 900,000 volumes, precious beyond description."

Amy is feeling sick: I blame you, old Father Raven. You should have sat among the smokers on the plane, given Alan the plague instead of me. Her mind is addressing Jiri under its breath: how dare you behave like that?

"The oldest volume in the collection is the Strahov Gospel-Book from the ninth century."

It's Josef returning in glory that he can't stand.

"During our tour, we shall be visiting two of the loveliest interiors in the whole of Europe, the Theological Library and the Library of Philosophy, among whose tomes, if I might be forgiven for mentioning a personal matter, is one written by my father."

Nobody ever awarded your dad a medal, though, is that it? Amy checks her mood. Steady on, sailor—who's being bitter now? You've got to understand how things are here.

The days of the pink tank are over.

Jiri is continuing, and forgetting that he is under instruction not to talk politics. "It is my prayer, ladies and gentlemen, that these treasures are not sold off to the highest bidder, like the rest of my country."

"Sold off?" responds Enid from Albuquerque. "Never!"

"Anybody with the cash—German, Japanese, Arab . . . we're broke, you see. Anybody can grab what he pleases."

He has tried not to look at Amy, but Jiri cannot prevent his glance searching her out. Is he having second thoughts about his outburst? "Forgive me," he says to the American tourists, "if I seem a little sensitive at this moment . . . about foreigners."

Dan from Wisconsin bellows out, "No need to apologize about foreigners, young fella—we don't like 'em either!"

Amy is remembering the more tender part of the troubled

persona of Jiri. She smiles to herself as she recalls him confess, "Sometimes I confuse being a guide with being a tram driver. On the Number 17 last week I found myself giving a talk about the Smetana Museum and half the passengers missed their stop."

That's the Jiri Amy wants to hold on to.

"You must be very proud of your father, Jiri," says Linda from Detroit. "Did he suffer under the Communists?"

"Oh yes—before . . . during." He pauses, giving his last phrase special emphasis. "And after . . . But he stood by his work to the end." Here Jiri's gaze is meaningful and once more finds Amy. "He did not renounce it. And for that, he suffered much."

"He wasn't one of those who was lustrated, was he, Jiri?" asks Melvyn, the attorney.

"What's it mean, Jiri," Sidney wants to know, "this lustration?" When Jiri hesitates, plainly flustered, head-shaking, Melvyn explains: "It means cleansing—purging. Smoking out the lackeys of the old regime."

"Not my father!" Jiri's voice echoes along the ancient walls of the Strahov.

"Of course not," soothes Betty. "I'm sure your father—"

"Is dead, Madam."

"Oh I'm so sorry!"

There is a moment's silence before Abe attempts to offer comfort to Jiri and relief all round, by saying, "But not forgotten, son, eh?"

Once more Jiri's eyes meet Amy's. "On the contrary, Sir, my father is absolutely forgotten!"

Amy is deeply grateful she is not Alice from Boston at this instant, who has been paying only partial attention to the conversation. "Well, Jiri," she says in total innocence, "so long as he wasn't disgraced . . ."

Jiri is stilled, robbed of words, head tilted back ever so slightly, and Amy feels a wrenching compassion for him.

Could it be?

He takes refuge in describing, ". . . richly carved book cases which came from the Bruch Abbey in South Moravia. The ceiling design is by Franz Anton Maulpertsch."

As Ned, the teacher from Vermont, notebook out, asks Jiri to spell the name, Amy Douglas turns her back on scenes depicting the intellectual history of mankind.

Time to go. I'm only a pain to him. He'll relax when I'm gone. In his presence it seems I remind him of things he doesn't wish to remember.

I'm the cinder in his shoe; only the cinder is splintered glass.

She is hurt by Jiri's accusation, particularly as she is not sure what the accusation is actually about.

Nothing figures, does it? I could punch him, I could kick him, but I know I'd end up kissing him.

So I won't do any of them.

By way of apology as she departs, Amy whispers to Iris from Kansas, "I'm sorry, but I'm really going to have to get this eye seen to."

"I don't blame you, my dear, my own feet are killing me."

Chapter Ten

Amy pauses in sunlight. Despite her mood, the vision of the city framed between these steep walls, the wrought iron lamp casting a shadow just above her head, and the dome of St Nicholas rising to her left, soothes her.

> *Prague never lets you go . . . This dear*
> *dear little mother has sharp claws.*

Dead right, Franz. I know what you meant. I could really love it here. She sits on the steps, against a railing. To her right, on a bare wall, someone has spray-canned the word HAVEL. Just that: not UP WITH; or DOWN WITH. Just HAVEL.

An epitaph? Jiri and Vera would think so.

They like their towers and their spiky bits, the Czechs; their clocks and their cobbled streets. And I'm bloody well going to enjoy them too. You, Jiri, are bitter and twisted. You're blaming Josef, and including me, for things that are nothing to do with either of us.

That's a coward's way.

Oh sure, I can understand some things. Dumping the past is fine if you've a future to go to. And you can see no future. Well what about me? I've not had much of a past. But for meeting Josef I'd have no present either.

I was a traitor too; to my calling. I gave up racing. "You were born to it." Oh yes, I trampled on my gift—but who was I doing it all for?

Huh, you can stick your school prospectus; the reports in the paper; the speech days when the head tells parents the school will very likely be represented at the Olympics.

Not for me.

So what have you got?

Well, you could say I got myself lustrated. I'm a non-person. Yet so long as I don't wake up one morning like poor Gregor Samsa, I'm content.

Half way down the hill to the Lesser Quarter, where the bridge-towers guard the western entrance to Charles Bridge, Amy buys an ice-cream and postcards of the city.

She is furious with Jiri. If they ever exchange words again, she'll have to say something about—what? Your arrogance. Of course it's not arrogance, and you know it.

What word would *you* use to describe it, Mrs A?

Amy pauses to look over Kampa Island, an area of tall houses and narrow streets looped by an arm of the Vltava and nicknamed Little Venice.

So beautiful; too good to last. Do you mean this—or us? Both. The ice-cream's terrific. Good music too; everywhere. Prague's a barrel organ, a hurdy-gurdy; you can't hear the wind for strings. That's not me speaking, it's Jiri. At least we've got that in common, though he knows ten times as much about music as I do.

"In Smetana's city, everyone is a music-lover. It's stamped in a Czech's passport."

Which reminds me, Josef's keen to go and hear the jazz. He pronounces it like it's a one-line poem of joy—*Djez!*

How he's changed. Yes, seeing that you're asking, Old Joe's what I've got.

The ice-cream finished, Amy examines the card she's selected for her friend Trish. On a huge grey-stone plinth stands a Russian C23 tank, pink as a wedding from gun barrel to caterpillar tracks.

She writes, cramming up the words:

> *Met this artthrob (joke, he's an artist) Jiri who painted tank in protest at war and occupation. If you beat a Czech in the pool, he's your slave for ever. Official! Prague purrs but no sign of Good Soldier Sveyk. Josef has sore ribs with laughing. He is toast of city. If we can keep him sober, all will be well. You'd love the Prague beer. J. calls it Pivo. PS. Jiri's taking me to The Bunker—hottest nightspot in town. PPS. Well, I hoped he would, but had heap big tiff. That's your Amy—opens gob and kills golden goose. Not to worry. I'll ask Josef to take Amy Kastov to the 'dzaz' instead!*

Amy also pens cards to JP, Mrs Benson and Mr Dodds. There's one of a naked male statue for Mrs Ambler, stating:

> *Since Velvet Revolution, the fig-leaf has been removed. Wish you were here! Amy Sveyk. PS. I'd appreciate your grandad's views on LUSTRATION—here, it's everybody's word-of-the-day.*

A few statues along on Charles Bridge, beneath the effigy of St Luitgard, three young recorder players are charming a crowd of people and pigeons. The girl in the centre of the group, with blonde hair brushed back from her forehead, is a dwarf. She plays the treble recorder with skill and a sombre expression.

Beside her, playing descant, is a girl of 12 or 13, wearing

a peaked cap. On her left is a boy playing tenor as if he had been born with it clutched between his fingers.

Amy laughs. The gaze of the young musicians is anywhere but fixed on the music in front of them. Their eyes soak in the world as it passes—and yet their playing is perfect. She drops the equivalent in Czech crowns of fifty pence into the hat. "Danke!"

What was it Vera said? "We are all Germans now!"

And it is at this moment that Amy senses she is being watched.

The feeling wasn't here before; it's here now, and strong. Reason says—don't be silly. That's why the crowd's here, to have a good stare. Anyway, being blonde, I get looks. Then they see how spotty I am and they don't look much longer.

Maybe it's the black eye.

Instinct ignores reason: Amy Douglas, you are being watched. She squats against the balustrade of the bridge.

Now who are you? A slow pan of the crowd. Nothing. Perhaps this feeling is something I've caught, along with Father Havran's flu. People here used to be followed and spied on so much that they could've left their anxieties floating in the air, like gnats.

One's just come in on the breeze from the river and bitten me.

Amy moves along, almost out of earshot of the musicians. She pauses under the statue of St John of Nepomuk.

If Amy's black eye were not so swollen, she would see directly opposite her a young man in the shadow of Sts Ludmilla and Wenceslas; notice him turn away from his view of her, gaze up river and then, very casually, and with a faintly perceptible limp, head for the tower guarding the route to the Old Town.

There, he stops. He resumes his surveillance of Amy Douglas.

She is noting a chill in the air. "I think it's going to snow!"

At the bridge entrance, the young man tucks himself out of sight at the arrival of Vera, running, swerving out from a pedestrian underpass.

"Oh—Amy!"

I should have known—something's up. Vera's out of breath, nose running. Amy offers tissues. "Amy—Oh God . . . I phoned the hospital. Just now. Your Josef has gone!"

"Gone?" At first Amy thinks—'gone' as in dead.

"He just walked out."

"Oh that!" The relief is terrific. For the moment.

"One minute he is there . . . I was so angry at them. They have searched the building. No sign—nothing."

"Was he dressed?"

"I think so."

"Well that's a blessing. So long as he's not wandering the city completely naked. I think it's going to snow."

"Does Josef wander?"

"Sort of. Especially when he's feeling better. At High Lawns he was in to hide-and-seek with the staff. But he always left a clue."

As they hurry off Charles Bridge they are watched; they are followed.

First, back to the hospital: Josef may have returned. They take a tram for two stops along the river. Amy tries reassuring herself. "He'll have looked out of the window, sensed spring in the air and gone for a stroll." Maybe.

Spring, what am I saying? It's about to snow.

Vera is looking at the young man who has boarded the tram behind them. She smiles because he is having difficulty punching his ticket.

"Don't worry. Nobody bothers. Dobra?" She does it for him.

"Dekuju!" Thanks. He returns Vera's smile, then moves to the back of the tram.

Vera asks Amy how the tour went this morning. Amy shrugs, glances away at the river. "You quarrelled; I guessed you would. Jiri quarrels with everyone these days. I was hoping you might be the exception."

"No such luck. Though it was probably my fault. I talked about Josef."

"He'll come round one day."

"From what? I mean, he's so full of himself."

"Not underneath."

"And why be so resentful of an old man?"

"Josef's in a long queue."

The first people they meet on the hospital steps are Alan Francis and his film crew. "Your Joe has vanished into the crystal air, Amy." Alan is relishing the occasion. He is a hound with the whiff of fox in his nostrils: a newshound on to a great story.

He is already seeing the future written in headlines: INJURED POET SNATCHED FROM HOSPITAL BED.

"Snatched, who said he's been snatched?"

Alan tugs at his newshound nose. "This says! What they want is the case—the locked case with the names. That's what they're after."

Amy stays calm. "If they're after the case, why abduct Josef?"

"Am I hearing this? Do I have to spell everything out to you in single syllables? Blackmail! Joe's life in exchange for the names."

" 'They'? What are you on about, Alan? Josef's gone for a walk. This is his home town, remember."

115

"Don't play the innocent with me, kidda." Amy now gets a mouthful about failing to put Alan and his crew in the picture about last night. "Apparently your black eye and Joe's crushed ribs are covered by the Official Secrets Act as rewritten by Amy Douglas."

Amy appeals to Alan's assistant, Sabrina. "Does your boss always go over the top?"

There is no need for confirmation. Alan is already over the top. Being shorter than Amy he moves up a step. "You, girl, are a bloody disgrace. All you're asked to do is keep an eye on the old duffer.

"When he gets his ribs caved in and his room burgled, what do you do, report it? The hell you do. Then you leave him in hospital and when somebody tries to take the matter seriously, what do you do, eh, what do you do?"

Amy tries to conceal her upset. Put Alan's way, she has been criminally neglectful. "Pandora's in the hotel safe."

"Pandora?"

"The box of troubles."

"Pandora—great! Note that down, Sab." Another headline forms: POET'S PANDORA'S BOX CONTAINS A PESTILENCE OF NAMES.

"And they, Madam Bloody Negligent, will want Pandora. Because you know what? The old bugger plans to read those names out—and what better time than the presentation ceremony when the whole of Czechoslovakia will be tuned in?

"Listen good, Amy. Your pal's life is in danger."

Amy is aroused enough to start pushing faces. "You are jumping to conclusions."

"Produce Josef Sabata for me, Amy, alive and well. Then I'll admit I'm wrong."

Bloody men! She's furious with Jiri, she's furious with Alan—but she's also annoyed with Josef. A kid, even though he might be a genius.

"I've already rung the London News Desk," says Alan. To his team, "And here's another nice angle for the folks back home: BRITS FEED POET FOR 20 YEARS. CZECHS LOSE HIM IN 20 HOURS. But not before letting him get beaten up, that is!"

These comments have at last got to Vera as well as Amy. "What do you want from us, a policeman on every tram?"

It is Vera's turn to be roasted, though Alan's words are for the Czechoslovak peoples as a whole:

"You Czechs've got dark problems, lady. PRAGUE PONDERS AS SKINS RUN WILD. And unless you do something about it quick you'll be up to your throats in Nazis before you can say Appy Adolf."

Amy takes Vera's arm, struggles to appear casual. "You've been reading too many spy thrillers, Alan. Josef's most likely gone out for some fresh air. He loves walking."

Not true, of course. Josef hates fresh air and detests walking; but he loves smoking and drinking. "I will speak to the doctor."

Alan still bars the way. "If Joe's been kidnapped, it's a matter for the police. Interpol, even."

Amy half believes him. It could happen. There's been too much mystery. "Listen, Alan. Will you give us till this evening? If we've not found him—"

"And what are we to do in the meantime?"

Vera: "Take a ride in an open carriage."

Eddie the cameraman likes the idea: "We could net some local colour, Alan."

Alan is always on about how movies have got to move. An open carriage-ride will not only get the camera moving, it will give it the shakes—which is what Czechoslovakia seems to be suffering from.

He agrees. "I'll voice-over. Yes, we'll go for the Kafka angle—Prague, a city in which nothing and no one is real, where the characters in our story wrestle with the nightmare of freedom."

Alan claps his hands together. "This is going to be a great piece. But first I want assurances from Miss Slippery Arse here. A promise, Amy, that you'll contact me at the hotel desk at six, pronto."

Anything to get rid of him. "Six o'clock, then."

"Promise!"

"I said—"

"I want the word!"

She promises.

It is old ground, talking to the hospital staff. Alan has done it all: Josef had had a restless night. The nurse put him back to bed at least twice. In the morning after seeing Amy he had asked to watch television.

"Football, please!"

He had been really pleased when they offered him a tele-recording of a Spartak match; not so pleased that they played a goalless draw.

"Then what?"

The distraught young doctor is almost in tears. "I have never lost a patient."

"No sign of struggle?"

"None. He had coffee served. Said his ribs were giving him hell, then we left him writing."

Despite a thorough search of the ward as well as the tele-vision room, no scrap of paper is found. "If it was any use, he'll have taken it with him."

"Not if he was kidnapped."

"You don't believe that, Vera, do you?"

"This country has had plenty of practice of that—in one way or another. That is how they took my father. At three in the morning, without leaving a goodbye note."

"If they were after Pandora, wouldn't they leave a ransom note?"

"Perhaps we sit beside the phone and wait."

Amy prefers to stick to simple explanations. "Josef is one big impulse. If he'd looked out of the window and seen the sunshine, he'd have asked himself, 'What the devil am I doing cooped up in this place?' Look, Vera, you know the city—where would an old poet head for?"

"Let's wander. We might become lucky." They emerge into the last sunlight of the afternoon, for grey clouds are advancing over the Petrin. "I think you are right, Amy—snow."

"Pubs," says Amy. She is sure of it. He wants his Pivo. "Sveyk loved The Chalice—how about starting there?"

No luck. The place is packed but in neither nook nor cranny is the poet Josef Sabata to be found.

"Alan may be right."

"There are plenty more pubs," says Vera, trying to keep Amy's spirits up.

In Amy's memory, something stirs. "Wait a minute!" She stops, closes her eyes. "Josef wrote this skit—in English, gave it me as a present. It lists a lot of pubs."

"A riddle?"

"How did you know?"

"Czechs love riddles. Do you have the poem?"

"I copied it into my notebook. It's at the hotel."

"Perhaps that is the clue you talked about?"

At Reception there have been no messages. Josef's

room has been tidied. Its emptiness suddenly saddens Amy profoundly. "I should have stayed with him, instead of . . ."

She ignores herself, leads the way to her own room and takes her notebook from the bedside table. "You know, we should've told the police. Interpol, even, like Alan said."

She adds, "What's more, I think I was followed this morning."

Out of the blue, Vera says, "Don't say you have fallen for Jiri."

"Fallen? What a peculiar expression that is." Amy is flicking through the pages of her notebook. "What's for sure is that Jiri's not fallen for me."

"You are probably what he needs, Amy."

"And I need his sort like a hole in the head."

"Read me the riddle."

Amy finds the page. Where are you, Josef, you old scandal? Come six o'clock, will we discover you're a martyr or a paralytic?

"Here we go:"

> *I leave my toes at Thomas's*
> *My dog at the Green Frog.*
> *I bequeath my medals at Bonaparte's*
> *My specs at the Fleks*
> *My bells at Schneks.*

"All pubs or wine bars," says Vera. "Go on."

> *At The Chalice I forget Alice*
> *My cares at the Little Bears*
> *But if it's my heart you're searching for*
> *Pass you by the Golden Tiger*

120

> *Seek no peace at the Mace*
> *You'll discover my perch*
> *At the sign of the Red Fox.*

Vera recognizes all but one of the references. Amy reads on:

> *Yet stay your pursuit.*
> *Go try a dram at the Two Cats*
> *For only a fool*
> *Would tell the Golam*
> *Of his Golden Well.*

"So?"

"He has said all the pubs—except his favourite one."

"Which one don't you recognize?"

"The Red Fox. As far as I know, there is not a Red Fox."

Without realizing it, Amy gives her friend a clue. "What rhymes with Red Fox?"

At once, Vera stands up, buttons her coat. She is smiling. "I think we take a tram!"

Chapter Eleven

Amy is disappointed it's not the Number 17 with Vera's hot-head brother at the controls. She has to settle for a Number 22 which takes them over the Vltava and up the hill. "All roads lead to the Castle, I see."

"Today they do."

Amy muses, old Kafka with his shivery stories is never farther away than the end of the street.

Suddenly all quiet, cobbles under foot, between white-washed walls, but not white—other colours, pale orange, sand, old stone; there's painted brick, never a window but it is decorated and different from its neighbours. Up steeply. We're behind a monastery or something. Could it be the Loreto again—described at length by Jiri this morning? Yes, she remembers the wrought-iron gates.

"Are we getting anywhere, Vera?"

A touch on the arm, a halt: ahead, a terrace of elegant three-storey buildings. "*Not* the Red Fox," says Vera. She points at a beautiful façade, with a sign over the modest entrance door. "But how about the Black Ox? The home of Pivo."

Through the door into another world: from silence to singing; from empty streets to packed benches. It's almost as if, at this time of day, the citizens of Prague abandon the city to tourists; and vanish.

Into the Black Ox.

"Here the best beer in all the world is sold," says Vera. "And poets come to recite the best poetry of Czechoslovakia."

They pass through the serving area and under an arch.

"Milacku!" One of the best poets in Czechoslovakia is standing on an oak bench at the bottom of the room, in mid-recitation, a crowd around him, still laughing at Josef's last comic rhymes.

For Amy, a great cloud lifts. She hugs Vera. It takes a Czech to read a Czech's riddle. "So much for the kidnap of the century!"

Poor Alan: this'll mean another call to his News Desk.

"Milacku—you found us!"

She grins, waves. "Tried the Red Fox but the beer was flat."

There must be thirty pilgrims of Pivo and poetry squashed in an area where fifteen would seem a crowd: plenty of long hair; earrings; beards—and tankards of beer frothing over the sides, some empty and screaming to be refilled.

Josef is tottering on the top of the table. "He's had a skinful."

In Czech, he introduces Amy to his friends and she's swiftly the toast of the Black Ox. "What're they saying, Vera?"

"They compare you to Stanley, entering the jungle to rescue Livingstone."

"Josef?" They are together. It is an embrace of warmth and love and relief. "You're drunk."

"Only tipsy, Milacku. I am happy. These are old friends."

"More, more!" chants the crowd.

Vera laughs. "They say Josef's poems make it seem like spring."

Prague Spring?

Amy is asking, for she is keeper of the purse (Josef never carries even a fifty pence piece), "Where did you get the money for the drink, Josef?"

"Everybody!" Another pint of this Pivo and he'll be under not on the table, Amy warns.

The waiter wishes to know if the girls want to order. "Of course," says Vera. "Two beers and sausages, please."

The beer is served in stout-handled glasses. There is a wicker basket of bread to go with the sausages. These are stubby and fat and clipped together. "Triplets."

Another beer and the poetry bird with grey head-feathers and flushed cheeks agrees to sing on. The audience is still now, quiet, carried into themselves as Josef's lines float through the smoke-filled room.

The beer is getting to Amy. She too is floating. Her eyes scan the walls of the Black Ox. There are knights with flowing headdresses. Everything twists and swims—tankards of frothy ale, hunters' horns, mountains of grapes.

She closes her eyes. The mustard and the sausages do for her what Josef's poetry seems to be doing for these old lags of Prague—prises open the past.

Back with her parents, mustard on the pie, a picnic in woods streaming with sunlight. She can hear the laughter now as they race between the firs and Dad trips on his face ten steps from the winning line.

Gone. In an instant, before you could shout "Slow down!"

"What's Josef saying, Vera?"

"You're crying."

"It's the beer . . . Forget it, tell me what he is saying."

"It's a poem called *Swimmers in the Snow*—"

"I guessed it was. It's for me—and him."

"For his country too, I think. The territory of his mind, he says . . ." Vera continues her translation: "Those that seek the truth—about themselves, about their place in things, must be as swimmers in the snow.

"For the snow is both the past and the future. All is struggle. Little makes sense. And thus in his mind he returns. To old abodes. Alas his passage is barred by a soldier who spins him round ten times."

> *Commits my mind and heart to darkness;*
> *Places my pen in solitary confinement;*
> *Seals my lips and pronounces me dead.*

Josef pauses. He drinks. He passes a hand over his face. His own words have affected him. No more comedy, no more jokes.

"I think he has forgotten . . . No, he goes on."

Amy's tears have also sprung from the past. She is remembering Josef Kastov, Sir Stubborn, who stared at a blank television screen and never said thank you. "What's he saying, Vera?"

"He asks—was the soldier himself, he the destroyer? Was the soldier bad faith? Could it be that the prison was of his own making? Who imprisoned his pen? *Who but I?*"

> *It is too easy to blame the enemy out there.*
> *The blood in the snow was spilled by my hands*
> *And the dagger was my silent pen.*

Another heavy pause. Another drink; and now a smile— that mischievous grin which had won Amy's interest and affection; so long ago, it seems at this moment, in another world, another life. "Now what's he saying?"

Vera is grinning too. "A new conclusion to his poem. He decided to dig up his old corpse . . . dust him down . . . give

125

him one glass of Pivo . . . put some flesh, some fat on him with Black Ox sausages . . . He is going to dance to the jazz— with you, Amy, till the dawn of the next century . . . What a stupid old corpse!—it knows it is alive because it want to pee."

Tears upon tears, but now tears of laughter.

Amy raises her almost-empty glass. "To swimmers in the snow, Josef!"

Without being ordered, two more beers land in front of Amy and Vera. Strange things are beginning to happen to the room. The mention of swimming has set off the walls and the ceiling; all are swimming.

A newcomer has asked Josef, "Where've you been all these years?"

He answers promptly, with a glance at Amy.

"What's he say?"

"That he ran away to a far distant country. And put himself into his own prison. Sleeping Beauty! The story go all wrong . . . And a young princess enter to give him a kiss—that's you. Raise your glass, they are all toasting you.

"The kiss it bring him back to life. Gives him hope . . . and honour in his old age . . . Mind you, he prefer no honour . . . Pivo is best—with good company!"

Pivo's best, true, and strong; and now the floor and the bench in front of Amy are swimming, out of unison, out of 'sync' with the ceiling and the walls.

Amy excuses herself, stands up, with the aid of the bench which does not seem so steady on its own legs any longer.

"You want help?"

"I'm okay."

"Let me take you—"

"No! I once swam the English Channel, I ought to be able

126

to make this crossing . . . Oh Vera, could you phone the hotel? I promised Alan."

"Do I tell him where we are? Better not, the Black Ox does not like reporters. It eat their notebooks."

This loo should be in a museum. I wonder, did the Good Soldier Sveyk plonk his bum on this very seat? I'm drunk. Josef's drunk.

Sorry, JP, this isn't what you'd call quality caring. You'd like the lampshade in here, Mrs Benson. Real fancy. Turn of the century, as Jiri would have to say. Which century? I'd have to say. And then he explains to me all about Art Nouveau.

And I say, if it's new, how can it be turn of the century? He touches my hand. I liked that. 'I *was* an art student.'

Now he's a tram driver. Funny old world.

Vera's going to have to carry me home. In an open carriage. I'd like that: clip-clop, clip-clop on the cobbles, under the pinnacles, under the spires, under the stars.

Hi, Jiri—shift your tram!

And Jiri lifts his tin of pink paint. "Can't you see it's a tank?"

Somebody knocking on the door.

"Okay. Coming." Trying the handle: no luck; pulling at it: no luck. Christ, don't say I'm locked in. "I'm sorry." Shaking at the door. All at once it is wrenched open.

"Out!" Above her stands an armed guard: a soldier in a green overcoat. A gun barrel is thrust towards her face.

"Out!"

Amy raises her arms: an automatic reaction. It is what she expected. What she has been groomed to expect. The soldier is joined by another. The square outside is full of them. She climbs into the covered truck. It is full of children, most of them younger than her.

They carry small cases or sacks full of their belongings. Opposite her is a boy wearing a Basque cap made of dark blue corduroy, a size too big for him. The neb shadows his face, but the shadow is not dark enough to conceal the fear in his eyes. She smiles. The boy's expression does not change.

The truck is full, moves off with a snarl of gears. There is a guard in the back, his gun trained on the children.

"I am Amy, what is your name?"

The command comes in German: "No talking!" Amy understands it. The boy does not wish to seem afraid: "Josef," he whispers. He glances to his right. "My sister, Ilona."

Ilona is afraid even to look.

As the truck winds down from the Castle, there is a glimpse in the dark of lights sparkling in the Vltava. It is to be a long journey. The city is left behind. The hills begin, rising out of woods. They pass through lightless villages; the air is strangely warm, summery and now they are climbing again, the truck in low gear; to another castle on a hill, and surrounded by low-lying houses. It is a walled town.

I have things at the back of my mind but I cannot bring them to the front. I am older, and they are looking to me. I have become a leader. Walls have closed around us. We are in ranks and there is a man reading off our names from a list.

"Professor". That is what he would prefer to be called, because it is what he once was. He is gentle and kind. One of us.

"Children, you will be in my care, and me in yours—for you must bear with me. I am not a school teacher, nor have I ever run a school of this sort."

It is a fortress: stone walls several feet thick; winding staircases; and slit windows overlooking countryside.

"You may call it the Castle. It is our home for the duration."

A difficult word. Josef's sister Ilona clings. "The duration?"

128

"For a time."

"Are we safe?"

"I hope," says the Professor, "that we will all be safe. Terezin is . . . er, out of the way. I pray too that we will be out of mind."

A sweet smile over spectacles. This man is as scared as we are.

Dormitories for the girls, dormitories for the boys. Josef at supper, "We are all Jews." It is in answer to another boy's question—"Why are we here?"

Amy makes no comment.

"There will be lessons as usual, don't think our stay here is going to be a holiday."

"No, Professor."

"What is your favourite subject, Josef?"

"Writing."

"And yours, Ilona?"

"Painting."

"And yours, Anna?" The question is directed at Amy.

"Swimming."

"We shall take you to the river one day."

Josef has edited his own magazine, with the help of friends; calls it *Rim Rim Rim*. According to the Professor it promises a glowing future for such talents. They are allowed one walk through the town on Saturdays. They go in parade with the German soldiers at front and back.

This day Ilona is happy. A child stepped from a side-street and handed her a tiny parcel. Inside was a polar bear with a black nose. "I shall keep it always."

Ilona paints her life and her loves in the art class. "What are they all doing?" asks Amy, pointing at the squirrel and the rabbit, the cat and the pig, the snail, the mouse and the hedgehog.

129

"Looking for Daddy and Mummy."

"Will they find them?"

"I think so. They will run about quietly, and the Germans will not see them. And they will come back with a message."

On another Saturday, a lady at the corner thrusts into Amy's hand a heart-shaped box. Later she finds inside a variety of coloured cottons. Hana receives; a reward for her painting of a black Scottie dog.

They are all standing in line in the cattle yard. The Professor says tomorrow there will be no school. "I am to be . . . transferred, children."

He tells them that they too will be taking a journey. "There is no information beyond that . . . You will be permitted only to take your absolute essentials."

At the back of the mind, a feeling. There are no words for it. The trucks arrive early. Shall we be together? Amy—called Anna—finds words in her head, words in her mouth:

"Josef, you must jump and run."

"They will shoot me."

"Jump and run!"

"I will not leave my sisters."

The phrase includes Amy.

"Jump and run," says Ilona without looking at her brother. Bitterly cold, a fog so thick it hangs like the smoke of wet bonfires even in the town streets. Jump and run—why not me? No, I am anchored here.

Amy has spoken: "Just one of us."

It has been a game of straws: each chosing one—Ilona, Josef, Liza, Margareta, Doris, Beta, Marika, Gertruda, Evan, Ruth, Hela; without exception: Irena, Egon, Edita, Nelly, Tomas, Marie, Lenta, Julie and Erika.

Josef pulls the shortest straw. And at the cross-roads, as planned, all the children begin to scream, and hurl them-

130

selves about the truck as if bitten by tarantulla spiders.

Traffic has slowed the trucks almost to a halt; and Josef jumps and runs. In the confusion, in the roasting shouts of the guards, he is not noticed. There will not be another head-count till journey's end.

The fog is all around. The guards beat up the tallest. Amy falls among legs. Her head bleeds. Her eye swells till the eye cannot see. They are transferred to railway trucks. There are others on board; grown-ups; and more to come till she is squashed so tightly she can hardly breathe.

Ilona is away down the truck, dwarfed by grown-ups. There is moonlight between the sliding doors and in here a stench, of sweat and urine and excrement.

The doors are slammed to and bolted.

At the back of the mind, something; but there is no language for it. No one talks, though some weep. Hold everything in. Remember the moonlight. Josef, how's freedom? Make the best of it, my little brother.

Ilona calls, "Let me through. Please—my sister!"

"We have all lost brothers and sisters."

No one shifts for her. No one *can* shift for her.

"One of the soldiers said they want workers in the factories."

"If you've a trade, you'll be all right, they say."

"I'm a musician."

"You'll be in clover. The Germans love music."

"One of them back there was quite kind. He smiled. He was offering my kid chocolate. Only the officer stopped him."

"Not all Germans hate us."

"The best thing is to do what we're told. Cause no trouble."

"I'm not sure. One of them called us sheep. But what did he want us to do, answer back, refuse to climb on board? He'd have shot us."

"We'll be safe if we keep together."

This comment causes laughter. "So you think we have a choice?"

Ilona could not reach Amy but Amy has pushed and nudged and shouldered her way to Ilona.

"Be content!" somebody snaps. "Who do you think you are?"

They are together now, holding each other tightly, heads together.

Something, something; at the back of the head.

They have not opened the truck even though the train has stopped.

"Why can't they let in some air?"

"Why can't they tell us something?"

And the train moves on; stops, waits an hour—two hours; moves on. And the heat is intense, the stench horrible. They are relieving themselves, but in an orderly fashion, in the corner. Yet some cannot reach the corner. No one can move. It has to happen this way.

Choking. Head pounding. No air. There are people falling. An old woman has no one. She was crouching in a ball. She rolls over, against legs which cannot release themselves for the crush.

"Is she ill?"

"She is dead."

"Somebody should call the guard." The train is stopped again. Outside, voices; commands. A delay. The old are lying down, surrendering the spirit. There are sick ones too; a child staggers into a stranger's arms and then slides to the shit-wet floor.

"Guard, guard! We're suffocating. Open the doors, please."

They have heard. Must have. But they do not open the

doors. They are smoking. Farther off, there is singing. The train moves on.

There are those sleeping standing up and those dying standing up. The train stops. There are endless calls for water.

I have nothing in the head. Nothing to help. And the train starts, speeds. There is no night and no day. Ilona sleeps; and in her sleep, emits a scream.

The doors are unlocked and flung open. "Down!" A morning, thick snow; all but the next few yards up the hill enveloped in mist.

"Halt!"

Ilona's hand rests tightly in Amy's till they are ordered to separate. "No touching!" A glance back, there must be four hundred of us. We are being divided into groups. I remember the station clock said six o'clock. It seems later than that. How warm everything looked through the windows.

No food, no water—but exercises. "That's a good idea," says a father easing his four-year-old down on to the snow. "It will put the life back into our bones."

Soldiers, all the way, with rifles pointing; and now the instructors. We are swinging arms. Back, back, up and round; back, back, up and round. Swing at the waist, one, two, three, four; other way, one, two, three, four. Bend at the waist, touch toes, one and two and three and—pause.

And now, face down. "Swim!" call the instructors. "Swim!"

There are those who cannot get up again. They have spent their last strength attempting to swim in the snow. Now they drown in the snow. They are beaten with rifles.

Finally the command is for running on the spot. "Up! Up! Raise those knees!"

When it is obvious the crowd can stand no more, the order

is given for the procession to continue up the hill. The father of the small boy says, "That will keep out the cold."

"They plan to keep us fit," says another voice. "That's something."

A child: "I liked the station. It was warm."

Yes, a fire in the hearth. They have issued us tickets. "For soap, I think they said it was."

Ahead, buildings which look like washhouses. "We need delousing all right."

There is a sense of relief. Anything will be better than those trucks. The doors are open. Changing rooms.

"You will take off all your clothes." The officer signals to a soldier at the end of a long counter. "You will be given a receipt for everything. Remove all jewellery too, and shoes."

Something at the back of my head; will not come clear.

"Ilona?"

"Keep in line."

"She is my sister."

"Keep in line! Clothes off, including shoes."

"Be sure to retain your tickets."

I can see some of the others now: Hana, Tomas, Marie. We are being directed through into another room. "Showers," says the father of the four-year-old. "But they've forgotten to issue us with the soap."

I turn, and the crowd has been stopped; and Ilona is behind me, lost in the queue. I shout, "Let her through, she's my sister!"

A soldier bars the way. "You will meet up on the other side. Be patient."

The door is shut fast. There are too many of us in here for a shower: and where are the showers? The room is bare concrete and I am smelling something. I am close to the door,

an iron door, a door that rings a little with my blows. "Ilona!"
I smash against the door. I beat it.

"Ilona!"

I cannot breathe so well. It is the shouting. But the smell is getting worse. Everyone smells it. They are panicking and I am not helping. I bang on the door with my fist. Now I am on my knees. I am choking, suffocating:

"Let me out!"

The door opens inwards and the lock goes spinning on to the floor.

"Amy, thank God!" Vera and the waiter lift Amy up from her knees. "Ilona!"

"What? Here, lean this way. What happened?"

"They locked us in."

"*They?*"

Suddenly wide awake; ill and dizzy and shaking, but—oh glory!—here and safe; held by tender hands.

"What happened?"

Too crazy to tell them. Later, when I can see straight and feel straight again. "I must've dozed off. I dreamt . . . I was swimming in the snow."

Chapter Twelve

Just in case a certain person calls from Reception and invites her to go swimming, Amy sets her alarm. *I am ill but I'm not going to let that spoil things.* She gazes at the clock face: six o'clock, the time registered by the station clock in her nightmare. She shivers. *It was so horribly real. Did the dream really tune in to Josef's childhood? It might explain a lot about him.*

I guess most of what I dreamt he's told me, in fragments, one time or another. Plus my reading; and Mrs A's rambling lessons. Nazi Germany was one of her pet subjects.

Amy moves the minute finger of the alarm clock on to six-fifteen. *Like my mum, superstitious.*

Earlier, Josef had insisted on returning to the hotel in an open carriage. The horse's breath made steam in the frosty air and so did Josef's, for he sang all the way.

Crossing the Vltava he insisted on a pause to give thanks to the River Goddess for allowing the Czechs to survive the Thirty Years War, Adolf Hitler and the drab parade of Communist leaders who'd have banned the flowers opening if they could.

"And now may the Czechs be preserved from the Slovaks, and the Slovaks from the Czechs!"

Amy and Vera needed two porters to help carry Josef to his room. The poet's last words before snapping into a profound sleep were, "I have just understood how Dodds cheats at cards."

Vera had been too tired to go home. But she had insisted, "You must come to our place before you leave, Amy. See what the tourist of Prague never sees."

"Nothing will surprise me," Amy replied. "Personally, I live in a bath."

Amy had another dream, not unlike what had really happened on Jiri's tour. The surprise was that he had called for her to go swimming—and then apologized. "I didn't think you would bother . . . After this morning, I mean."

Even in a dream she has no intention of going easy on Jiri. "You made accusations, about Josef and me—"

"Not you. You have nothing to do with it."

"That's not the way it came over."

"All I'm saying as far as you are concerned, Amy, is that you have probably been taken in by your wonderful friend Josef. He is not what he seems—believe me."

"He jumped from the back of a Nazi truck, you know. That's how he survived."

Jiri fails to register Amy's comment. "You see," he continues, "I don't like my friends being deceived. How do you say in English?—taken for a ride."

"Friends? Who said we were friends?"

"What is it with you English?"

"Tell me."

"You must always have the last word."

"Don't you mean English women? They stand up for themselves."

"No, *that* I admire."

Amy doubts this. "But if they're to be *your* women you want them to be a bit more . . . subservient?"

How about that word, Mrs A, after three pints of Pivo and a trip down memory lane?

Mrs Ambler seems glad to join Amy's dream. "If I were you, young lady, I'd stop spending all your time gassing with this fabulous male torso and join him inside the Pink Tank."

"I don't make love in the back of tanks, pink or otherwise."

"More fool you, Amy."

"What is it with you married women, Mrs Ambler?"

Jiri has other things on his mind than the Pink Tank. For a moment she thinks he is folding his arms around her in the swimming pool. Instead he is wrestling her arm into a half-nelson.

It's what happened when the police arrested her and Spen. Left arm right up the back until I thought my shoulder would break.

"Amy, I want those names!"

In the dream, the magistrate from Amy's first court appearance stands up from his seat and pounds the bench in front of her. "We want the names!"

Who should turn up next but JP. "The names, Amy. This is a public company now. Our creditors are demanding the names or they will cut our funding."

Mr Dodds places four aces in front of her on the table. "Beat that hand, and then tell me Sir Stubborn isn't a spy!"

The turret of the pink tank is open, and inviting. Amy in her dream slips inside. Jiri is sitting there, quite naked; but so are his American tourists. They all look terrified.

Abe from Nebraska speaks for the rest. He is trembling. He says, "They've discovered we're Jews, Anna. Can you help us?"

At the corner of the Jewish Cemetery, just outside its walls, there is a tiny museum on three floors. Its exhibition rooms are scarcely big enough to accommodate more than a dozen visitors at a time.

From a window on the first floor Amy Douglas stares out over the gravestones—thousands of them, grey and green-stained from the trees; sprouting from the ground like slab-shaped plants. There are so many graves they seem stacked upon one another, fighting for space.

She thinks, fighting for remembrance.

Alan Francis and his film crew are down there now. It will all look good on film—Josef strolling poetically through sun and shadow, pausing, counting his ancestors (though he's told Alan his ancestors are buried in Bratislava).

"Who cares?" Alan had replied. "All art is an invention."

This comment had rather impressed Josef. He understood: okay, he would pretend to search for his non-existent ancestors in the Jewish Cemetery of Prague.

Poetry too is about illusion.

Jiri had not called. Amy had thought of going for a swim on her own. Instead she turned over and had to be wakened up by Vera, with Alan rattling at the door and insisting on an early start.

She has only come in to the museum to escape the cold yet look—tears. Thank God I'm alone. Nightmares have a habit of repeating themselves, who doesn't know that?

Vera recommended this visit. The museum houses the possessions of children—drawings, paintings, hand-produced newsletters. Nothing nightmarish about that, except that these are the last marks made on earth by Jewish children taken from the fortress of Terezin; before their journey to the railway station.

Where the time is always six o'clock.

Yet nothing of what is displayed before Amy in modest glass cases is new to her. Did I truly dream all this? Or are

139

these items traces of memory from my reading? Did Vera talk to me about it in my sleep? I am feeling sick now, and depressed.

Ilona Weissova. Born 6th March 1932. Taken to the camps. Died 15th May 1944. Did you change your name, Josef? Or is this another Ilona?

Before me is Ilona's drawing: a squirrel, a rabbit, a cat, a pig, a snake, a mouse, a snail and a hedgehog. It is all here. Greetings from the living. To you, Hana Beckova, who also died 15th May 1944, aged 14—remember the coloured cotton?

Greetings to you all here—Marit, Liza, Margareta, Doris, Beta. So this is what happened to the polar bear with the black nose. Does Josef know any of this?

Well, Alan, you're in the wrong location. Sure, the gravestones make a good picture. You'll get a prize for your documentary. But it's here you ought to be filming. This is the true story.

What's more, Josef is leading you a dance: are you leading us all a dance, Josef?

In the night there has been a flurry of snow. The air has become grey, the clouds dense. A leaf has blown against the pane and stuck in the frame. There is a breeze and it wrenches at the leaf, won't let it go, but nor will the leaf give up its grip.

Amy finds she has no tissues to wipe away her tears. She uses the back of her hand. Suddenly aware that she is being watched, she turns. But she is alone, though she hears footsteps on the stairs to the ground floor.

Weeping for the dead—that's rich. She continues to stare out. There are tourists in goodly numbers now roaming the cemetery. Vera's new group of Canadians from Toronto is due.

"Don't you get bored telling them the same thing over and over again, Vera?" Amy had asked her.

"That's it, I don't. I tell them what they want to hear. They are looking for roots, any roots. So I tell them, yes, someone of your name is buried here."

"Does that make them happy?"

"No, it makes them sad." A grin, "But satisfied!"

"Graveyards are morbid."

"Don't you visit your own parents, your Auntie?"

"Visit them? They were cremated. Of course not."

"Oh, that explains the difference. You weren't born in a land where people went missing."

The tragedy of Czech history is met here, in the pictures that have moved Amy to tears: the Nazi terror; and of the Communist terror which succeeded it; both created by religions that tolerated no doubts, no questions.

"If you did not join in the May Day parade," Vera had said, "they came to hunt for you. Jiri refused."

"So they kicked him out of college?"

"Oh no. Because of my father, Jiri was barred from college. Me too, of course."

"Yet you're so well educated—both of you."

"Do you have the same proverb in English?—there are more ways than one to skin a hare?"

Amy has never been hot on proverbs. "Tell me about your father, Vera."

"He spoke out. Against the danger of our nuclear power stations. They silence him. They say, 'Your job is yours again—if you recant'."

Recant? Another new word, Mrs Ambler. Didn't Christians who preferred not to become martyrs do that? "Apologize to the State. Beg forgiveness and promise never to do it again."

Thanks, Mrs A. Whatever would I do without you?

"What's wrong with an empty apology?"

"Because after the apology, they say, 'Tell us about your friends'. You say one word—and your friends go to prison. Or perhaps they die."

"Were you ever asked to report on Jiri?"

A smile. "Oh, in that respect, Czechoslovakia was the land of opportunity."

"Was he asked to report on you?"

"I think so."

"And did he?"

"For certain, I shall never know . . ." A shrug. "After the Velvet Revolution my father, he should have honour for his courage. Instead, someone made an accusation, that he collaborated with the Secret Police. He killed himself one year ago. On Christmas Eve."

Silence. This room is so silent it seems to tune the ear into the whispers of history. "No wonder Jiri is so bitter . . . But if your dad had the courage to stand up to the Communists, how come he didn't go on fighting when all he had to beat was a lot of soft democrats?"

Another shrug. "How do you fight old friends when they accuse you? In those years, only the dead were innocent. But you would not understand."

"Maybe not, but let me try, okay?" Amy had waited, curbed her impatience and then asked, "And your mother?"

"She was an actress, not famous, but good. When my father suffered arrest—given seven years—she was not any more permitted to work at the theatre.

"The only job she was allowed was at a flour mill. She carried sacks for eight hours per day. She died two months before Dad returned from prison."

Another silence, another space.

"Can I come with you, to put flowers on her grave?"

"I thought you hated graveyards."

Amy had replied, "I've no history, Vera. I'd just like to share a little of yours."

Amy bucks up at the prospect of Alan's next film location: it's the Kavarna Slavia, scene of a certain happy and untroubled breakfast with a certain tourist guide.

Where are you, painter of the Pink Tank?

Alan has pitched endless questions at Josef. At the same time he has done most of the answering himself. "We want to know details of your past, Josef. Where you were born. What happened to your family. You're Jewish, your bruised ribs remind you of that. Tell us how you survived the war?

"You were anti-Communist. How many years did you spend in prison? How did you survive until your breakdown? Exactly how did you reach Britain? Who funded you? Were you persecuted—they say the StB even tried to kill you in London, because they suspected you had the names of those who invited the Russians to crush the Prague Spring with their tanks, hence your shift to Clacton.

"Tell us, Josef, about your case—Pandora. Do you feel you are still in danger? After all, Czechoslovakia's split down the middle over whether the criminals of the past should be punished or forgiven."

From Josef, nods, smiles, winks. He is probably thinking of the Black Ox; carried from there, drunk as an ox, singing an old Slovak lullaby taught him by his mother.

"It was in the Czech papers today, Josef. The country awaits . . . Will you open Pandora when the President makes you the award? Questions, questions, Joe—people want the answers."

Josef drinks his Pivo and gives nothing away. He has grinned. He has answered in riddles. He has performed better than a circus seal. And Alan has not been especially displeased. Prague has set the scene. History has given him facts. Others have filled in detail. The rest is for Alan to pack with his own interpretations, his own fantasies.

"Communism drained the soul, right? But tyranny and terror—they are good for art." He talks to camera. "Look at this old poet. He is rock; he is granite. Authority has tried its damnedest to destroy him, but he has out-lived its interrogators, its tanks, its water cannon.

"His words will out-live the jackboot." Good, Alan likes the phrase. "What do you think, Sabrina?"

"A prize-winning remark, Alan."

"I'm inclined to agree with you . . . Joe, one last question remains uppermost in the mind. You have never mentioned your family. Not a word. But the papers claim you had a son."

In Amy's head at this moment is the picture of Josef on Wenceslas Square, defying the tanks; and carrying a child on his shoulder. The boy wears a Basque cap and carries a placard.

"No son!"

That is how Amy had been answered when she dared ask. "No son!" And then a revelation: "Dead!"

Alan Francis is not entirely without feeling. "Okay, rest easy." He has a small boy of his own. He shifts his line of questioning. "What we have to know, though . . . what the people of Czechoslovakia have to know—and our own people back home, who sheltered you under their wing for so long . . . and take your time in answering . . . what we have to know is—how did you come by those names?"

Josef downs the last of his Pivo. He is becoming locked into himself. "No names! Nothing."

144

"So you carry round an empty case?"

"Alan," begins Amy, warningly.

"Okay, okay. Let's get another beer."

"No names!" repeats Josef.

Amy longs to be away, walking beside the river. I just want to disappear into the mist over Petrin Hill. But Josef's well into another tall glass of Pilsener which is helping him forget the pain in his ribs.

So long as Alan doesn't ask about his son or Pandora, Josef is happy to share his smoke-filled memories of a time when, as he put it, "You could not fart without being arrested for insulting Comrade Stalin."

Amy stares out, sad. It will all be over so soon. Then back to High Lawns or the dole queue; to Mr Dodds demanding to be washed.

A tram passes. Amy hadn't realized how much the sight of trams excites her. Outside, at the bridge corner, the traffic lights have changed to green.

However, the Number 17, bright blue, with a yellow camel on its side, stays blocking the view. All at once there is a face at the Slavia window and a fist knocking the glass.

Jiri is signalling her to come out. Take a tram ride. He points. He's holding up the traffic. He taps his watch.

Don't take all day deciding.

You should give him two fingers and turn away. But Amy's head isn't ruling the rest of her today. "Josef—that's the guy who painted the Pink Tank. He wants me to help him paint his tram another colour."

She kisses her old friend on the forehead.

Josef stares out at Jiri. He nods, pats her hand.

"Hey, Miss Douglas," protests Alan. "We haven't finished with you."

All Amy can think of saying is, "That person owes me money."

Sabrina laughs. "Go for it, Amy. You're not likely to meet a better-looker for a long time. And don't worry—I'll steer Josef back to the hotel."

"Thanks, Sabrina." To Josef, "I'll be home before six, Milacku. In plenty of time for the ceremony."

Amy sprints between the café tables, out, turning right towards the river. It is like a relay race. Jiri has come to fetch her, grasps her hand, holds up the traffic. Together they spring aboard the Number 17.

To the restless passengers, Jiri calls, "British tourist—Very Important Person. Olympic swimming champion!" And then, "Smetana Museum next stop!"

Chapter Thirteen

"How do you say in English? I will show you my etchings."

Amy laughs. "That's what you don't say in English."

"But I do have etchings—really. All my own work."

The apartment in Kobilisy district had belonged to Jiri's parents. Now Vera and he share it. "Once upon a time, under the Nazis, this was a place for executions."

A new driver has taken over the Number 17 from Jiri. They walk a steep hill overlooking an industrial area of the city. Amy tells Jiri about her nightmare, of being arrested, forced on to a truck and taken to Terezin.

He shows no surprise. "There were so many horrors. They hang in the air. Even innocent tourists don't escape them."

Jiri stops at a small confectioners and buys pastries. Outside again, he says, "The woman who served us—her grandfather and three of his brothers were taken and shot, with about two hundred others. Just down the road from here.

"That was after Reinhard Heydrich, the Hangman of Prague, was murdered during the war. Blown up in his open car by freedom fighters parachuted in from your country.

"You've heard of Lidice? They shot every male in the village. Reprisal. The women and kids they sent to the concentration camps."

"Not just Jews, then?"

"Czechs, Slovaks—it did not matter. Only two assassins, but all of the Czech nation was guilty after that." Jiri shrugs. "Still, we Czechs are a forgiving people. Now we sell off the country to the grandsons of the soldiers who filled our streets with blood."

"Better business than bullets, though."

"If the business belonged to the people, I'd say yes. But employers, they have much in common with the Nazis."

"So Communism wasn't all bad?"

"Bad for some. Good for many. But the tyranny—that spoilt everything."

"You can't force people to be good."

"At least under Communism nobody had to sleep in a cardboard box."

"Maybe you'll come and visit me in my bath sometime, Jiri. You can sleep at the tap end."

Their hands clasp. "But no races!"

They walk on and Amy points at a splendidly ornate tower on the opposite side of the road. "Another fairy tale?"

A dome crowns the tower and surmounting the dome is something resembling one of Jiri's pastries, with a globe on top and a pinnacle on top of that.

Am I referring to the tower or to us?

Jiri smiles. "It has survived Nazi occupation, Communist rule, Russian occupation. Nobody dares touch its magic . . . As a kid, when I was depressed, I would draw the tower or sketch it in watercolour.

"It always looks different—as the light changes, in winter, in spring."

"A tower for all seasons?"

"It will even survive the partition of my country."

She is wondering why Jiri cannot bring himself to be more

friendly towards Josef. After all, both of them view the splitting of Czechoslovakia into warring halves as a tragedy; a pointless, tragedy.

Instead, she puts her arm around Jiri's waist; something she has wanted to do ever since he lost the swimming race yesterday morning; but won her approval.

The apartment comprises the ground floor of a four storey building. The stairs and the walls are of stone. The door echoes in the stone as it bangs, and feet resound up the winding steps. Somewhere above them a baby cries and its voice too echoes in the stone.

A little bit of High Lawns follows you everywhere.

"Could you live in a dump like this, Amy?"

"Dumps are my speciality."

The ground floor window overlooks a small garden dominated by two apple trees. "There is my father's shed. He relaxed by making things. Renovating an old motor cycle. It is still out there. I only go in there when I want to cry."

The apartment is warm, clean, and crammed with remembrances—pictures of Jiri's father and mother; cuttings from the world's press—photographs of the Russian tanks in Wenceslas Square; of the student protests which finally forced the regime to deliver up its power.

Stacked against two walls in the sitting room are Jiri's paintings. They too record crowds in protest. There's the jet of water cannon turning a helpless crowd into a broken wave of shocked faces and upraised hands. There is a prison cell lit only by a candle stub and, in the corner, almost half out of the picture, are the stark eyes of a prisoner in deepest shadow.

He sighs. "Not very cheerful."

"There's nothing in pink, Jiri."

"Oh . . . the tank was a mistake."

"On the contrary, painting the tank pink must have given people hope."

He is not convinced. "Made the world laugh at us."

"No. It made the world laugh at tanks. That's got to be good."

He is not fully persuaded, but he smiles. "You have a talent for making people feel good, Amy. Your Josef Sabata is indeed a lucky man."

Jiri makes coffee and they eat the pastries.

Would you believe it? I think he's scared. "Plenty of paintings, Jiri," says Amy, "but no etching so far."

He clears his throat. "No. In fact . . ."

"In fact—don't tell me, you're out of etchings?"

"Well—"

"Given them away to your other women, have you?"

"Other women? No. Listen."

She listens, he says nothing. She hears her heart thumping. If we stop talking he'll be able to hear it too; unless of course he's deafened by his own.

Hope so.

This is different from Spen. Talk was never his thing. He simply launched himself in your direction. No finesse but plenty of passion. This is different. We need time and we haven't got much of it left.

Still, we've come this far. Will I have to launch myself at him or will we meet half way?

I just mustn't start giggling.

"Amy?"

"Yes?"

"I want you to know something."

"There is no need for me to know anything."

Silence. This is rushing it. Go on in this dumb fashion and you'll put the guy off for ever. Why doesn't he just say, "The bed's in there—like to try it?"

"Oh yes, on one thing I have to make—"

"Yourself clear?"

"Yes."

Either he's brought no protection or he doesn't fancy me after all. Bloody spots!

"I have got to say this . . ."

He suspects I'm not a genuine blonde. Bloody cheek!

"*We* are friends, Amy. But it does not mean your friend Josef is my friend."

"You've already told me that."

"So long as there is no misunderstanding."

"Good. Now was there anything else?"

"Anything else?"

"Look, Jiri. I came here to look at your etchings. You've shown me nothing but oil paintings and watercolours."

Somebody has to get us out of this pit of words. And if he takes me literally I'll kick him where it hurts, honest I will.

Mercifully Jiri is intelligent enough to muster a decent pass in the I-think-I-know-what's-going-on-here test.

"Back home, you have a boyfriend?"

"You asked me that—does it matter?"

"Of course. You English girls—you have a reputation."

"I have a friend called Dodds. He likes me to bath him— and scrub his willy with a backbrush."

Jiri laughs. "And sometimes he asks you to beat him with the handle?"

A shake of the head. "There I draw the line."

"I'm glad!"

"Then kiss me!"

*   *   *

151

Borne on a sharp wind, snow whirls about two walkers beside the river; Josef wheezing yet refusing to remove the fag from his mouth.

"I warned you," says Amy, coat zipped up past her ears.

A grin from Josef who has insisted on this sortie into the storm. "Too much TV," he has said, referring to Alan and his crew.

He had peered into Amy's face when she returned from her afternoon with Jiri. "Happy?"

A nod.

He seemed to have guessed everything. "Czech men— good lovers, eh?"

No comment: no need.

"Slovaks not so good. Okay, but less damn moody." He squeezes her arm. "I like the boy. But all the world on his shoulders, right?"

"Sort of. He's called Jiri. His father was a scientist and a philosopher. Died of disgrace. That makes Jiri very bitter. I don't know why—maybe he hates poets—but he has got it in for you."

"Got it in for me?"

"He resents you."

"Of course."

"But why?"

"Drink?" That's as much as Josef wishes to discuss.

"Well I hope he doesn't try to spoil things for tonight."

"Ah yes, tonight. Speeches! Ceremony! I spit on them."

"You will do no such thing. You will receive your honour with grace. You owe it to High Lawns and to me."

The old man hums, smiling, enjoying the snow in his face.

"Josef, I want you to promise me something."

"Anything, Milacku."

"Don't read out any names tonight."

"No?"

"Is that a question or a statement?" She waits. "Are you listening to me, Josef?"

"Of course, Milacku. And I also listen to my heart."

The snow is easing off. There is a crisp and even layer along the pavement. The bridges, the roofs stepping-stoned up to the Petrin and the dome of St Nicholas emerge from the darkness in white outline and white blur.

They drop in to the café of the Smetana Museum.

"I'd appreciate a straight answer, Mr Sabata."

He will always be Sir Stubborn. There is that old wicked twinkle in his eye. "Poets do not give straight answers, Milacku. Only businessmen and politicians—and they lie."

In the café people recognize the long-lost poet Josef Sabata; and they also seem to recognize Amy Douglas, in the words of *Prognosis*, an English language newspaper, 'The girl who made it all possible'. The paper has even uncovered Amy's criminal record, so there is a neat balance to the whole story: Josef returned her favour—and rescued Amy from a life of crime.

There is much shaking of hands. "Welcome home!" And questions to the wise old man: "Do you agree with this lustration business?" "You are a Slovak, do you wish for separation?" "Do you think the Germans will take us over?"

Separation, it is the fear of everyone, for the spectre of Yugoslavia, its descent into barbarous chaos and bloodshed, haunts every mind.

And all the while Josef gently protests, "I'm just a poet— just a poet." And to Amy, "Not a saviour."

Father Havran is waiting for them at the hotel reception. He still looks ghastly. Josef takes his arm and escorts him into the bar, orders glasses of Bechers. The priest is full of apologies. "I am so sorry I have been unable to act as your host. This flu, you see . . . So sorry."

Josef comforts him. "Do not worry, Father. The Lord sent his angel, the BBC, to look after us."

"The bad news," says Father Havran, for the moment forgetting his calling and downing the Bechers in one gulp, "is that the President himself has gone down with acute flu."

"Good, then we go to the Black Ox instead."

"No, no, Josef. The ceremony will continue as arranged. The Tomas Masaryk Award will be made by the Minister of Culture . . . There will be time to meet the President later."

"Tell him—Black Ox, or nowhere!"

"Vera, he's drunk!"

"Oh God—can he stand?"

"With me propping him up. He must have ordered another bottle. Josef says the last thing he wants to do is go and shake hands with a lot of snobs."

"Snobs?"

"Well, Ministers . . . You've got to help me get him dressed. Father Havran's due back in half an hour."

Vera says, "Alan and his gang are waiting outside for a big send-off."

"He wants me to say he's ill. In fact, I think he's caught Father Havran's bug. Which makes two of us . . . What's so funny?"

"All this. It is the curse of poets when you give them medals. They prefer to get high in the Black Ox."

"That's the only thing stopping him just going to bed. I said, No ceremony, no Black Ox afterwards."

They go to Josef's room. His trousers are around his knees. "Help, please," and he is lying half on the bed, half off it.

While Amy sees to him, Vera phones Reception and orders a pot of black coffee.

"Pull yourself together," Amy tells Josef. And then laughs, it's such a stupid thing to say. "Or at least pull your shirt down. What do you think this is, High Lawns on New Year's Eve?"

Josef is finally dressed, looking at himself in the mirror. "There," says Amy, "all the smart ladies will fall for you." The coffee is working a minor miracle. Perhaps he was only pretending.

"Are we all ready?"

Fingers crossed he forgets something—in the shape of a shabby old case. We can do without Pandora's Box at present. There are enough crises hurling about our heads.

But Sir Stubborn is not Sir Forgetful. "My case," he says, utterly sober it would seem. "I need my case."

"It's locked away in the hotel safe, Josef. Surely—?"

"I want it with me. Please!"

"You'll look ridiculous—with a case in your hand."

He is firm and closed:

"No case, Milacku, no ceremony!"

Chapter Fourteen

The kidnap of the poet Josef Sabata takes place at precisely 7.05 pm, fifty-five minutes before the Tomas Masaryk Award Ceremony is due to commence in Hradcany Castle.

At 7 pm Josef is upright, steady, in his glad-rags; looking, in Amy's view, the very picture of a poet. And her new trouser-suit, of navy with white flashes at the collar and sleeves, makes her look twenty-five and the very picture of— as she put it to herself in the mirror—A Reformed Criminal.

Vera is looking pretty good too, certainly in Josef's eyes: "If I had a son," he has said, "I'd like you for a daughter-in-law."

"What about me?" Amy had mildly protested.

"You—I choose for daughter!"

The chauffeur of the official car stands impatiently, nervously at the Reception desk. Vera translates his concern: he has had to park round the corner, which means leaving at a side entrance.

Strange, no sign of Alan and his gang.

Together they follow the chauffeur down rear steps and out into a poorly lit sidestreet. The car is not so grand. At first Amy thinks it's another Trabant, but then realizes it is the familiar Skoda. The bloke next door to Auntie once had one.

"I thought we were being treated to a limo," she says.

So did Vera. "It must be the cuts."

They are inside the car, Josef with Pandora on his knee; and there is another person in the front with the driver.

They turn right and then left along the Vltava. They cross the river and then swing left.

Vera says, "Excuse me . . ." There is no reply. "Excuse me, but it should be right for the Castle."

No answer.

She persists. "Driver, this is taking us to Smichov."

The man in the passenger seat turns round. He is wearing a plastic mask, the face of a tiger. He speaks in Czech.

"Oh no!" Amy does not require a translation. "Don't say we're being—"

"Quiet!" That's in English, but Tiger Face's instruction continues in Czech for Vera to translate. "We must keep still, say nothing and do exactly what we are told."

This stings Amy. She's never done what she's told. *Asked* yes, but *told* no. "You tell them to stop this car at once, Vera."

Vera is silent. Amy follows her gaze. The gun in the hand of the passenger is not a leftover from last night's dream.

"Oh . . ." She whispers now, "What's it all about, Vera?"

Vera translates the next comment from Tiger Face. "They will not harm us. But they must have the case."

Josef, usually so laconic (laconic, Mrs Ambler? Meaning 'of few words'), now bursts like a dam. The first words Amy understands perfectly: "Nay, nay, nay!"

"What's he saying, Vera?"

"That there is nothing within his case of the slightest interest to anyone but Josef Sabata. And that nobody in this world will open the case or take it without his permission."

"All right. If this is what Josef wants . . ." Amy suddenly reaches forward and grasps the driver round the neck. His peak cap tumbles over his face.

Tiger Face has the revolver in his left hand and is thus awkwardly placed to direct it at his prisoners in the back seat, unless he kneels and turns round.

Before the man can do that, Josef, usually as listless of body as he is laconic, lifts Pandora and uses it as a battering ram. At the same time he shouts something about the second battle of the White Mountain.

The gun goes off. The bullet nearly takes the driver's nose with it; shatters the driver's side window. The car is now veering into the tracks of a Number 14 tram. Amy lets go her grip of the driver.

Josef has decided these are police. "Bastard cops!"

"Tram!" scream Amy and Vera together.

For a second the driver seems more concerned about putting his hat straight than avoiding a head-on collision. Perhaps he does not recognize the tram, fails to discern that a vehicle that is not painted cream and red can nevertheless be a Prague tram.

At the last instant he wrenches his gaze from the Pepsi-Cola sign heading towards him and turns the steering wheel half round. The car grazes the tram.

Everybody yells with shock as if the accident had actually happened. The driver relaxes, throws up his hands in relief. He crosses himself. And the car heads for the pavement.

Amy thinks he has gone into a coma. She lunges for the steering wheel. Josef has knocked Tiger Face's gun from his hand. He is fishing for it now between his legs.

Once more the driver acts at the last instant. The car is going for a pavement lamp post. It swerves, but a fraction too late. There is the crunch of lamp post against front bumper, the shattering of a headlight. A parked car completes part one of the Second Battle of the White Mountain.

The collision is with a Trabant (Amy prays it's not the one Jiri borrowed from his pal, Max). Both vehicles lock in a crumpled-metal embrace.

Alan Francis has never had luck like this. Until the Josef Sabata story he has paddled in the shallows of telly success. But a kidnap!

Sabrina had been the one to spot the chauffeur escort Josef, Amy and Vera out through the side entrance to the hotel.

A hot chase has followed, camera whirring and Alan giving the commentary of his life. "Prague—in the fast lane! Kafka's Prague: what is real? While all the dignitaries await the arrival of—watch it, Sab! Keep the bloody steering wheel straight!"

"It's these trams!"

"While all the dignitaries gather in the marble halls of the presidential palace, trembling for the future of the Velvet Revolution . . . Slow, Sabrina. Just keep our heroes in sight . . . On the underside of revolution there is . . ."

"They're all over the road!"

Eddie: "I gotta change film!"

The rear door of the kidnappers' car is open and Josef has tumbled out on to the pavement, still grasping his case. Amy has received an elbow in her undamaged eye. She falls back into Vera.

The chauffeur has meanwhile begun to chase Josef; and Josef has run across the street, between two passing trams, with Pandora held above his head as if he expects tiles to fall from a nearby roof.

"Oh no—why doesn't he drop it?"

Sabrina slams on the brakes, swerves towards the pursuing chauffeur; hits three parked bicycles instead.

Alan: "Everybody out!"

They are in the middle of the street, running. Eddie puffs, "The pictures'll be black as thunder."

Alan puffs, "We'll re-enact the whole show later."

Tiger Face is now in pursuit of the chauffeur who is also pursued by Amy and Vera; while Alan and his crew are close on their tails.

All at once the gunman sees the film crew. "That's him!" yells Alan. "Stop thief!"

Tiger Face reacts in horror at the prospect of appearing on British television. Another tram screens him from his pursuers and when it has passed, the gunman has evaporated into the gloom of a sidestreet.

The chauffeur has meanwhile caught up Josef. He has snatched Pandora from him and pushed him into a doorway. He runs with the case, towards the river.

Amy and Vera pick Josef out of the leftovers of a vegetable stall. His nice new suit is flecked with bits of cabbage. "Milacku—my case!"

"Forget the case—are you all right?"

He wails like a baby who's had a favourite toy ripped from his clutch. "The case!"

No choice. "Don't say it, Josef—no case, no ceremony." Amy sprints after the chauffeur, catching up Alan's crew—who've wined and dined a little too heavily for half-marathons—and passes them.

"Hold everything till we get there!" commands Alan through bursting breath.

Thank God I decided against the high heels.

There are scarcely thirty yards between Amy and the chauffeur now.

Amy shouts, "Drop that case!"

One glance over her shoulder confirms that Josef hasn't

drunk too much Bechers to prevent him rejoining the race. He is tugging Vera along behind him.

The chauffeur has reached the riverside. He crosses the road, turns, sees Amy; behind her, staggering but invincible, Josef; behind him, Vera; behind her, the film crew, all shouting "Shop Beef!" or something like that.

He hurls Pandora over the river wall and into the darkness below. He bellows at his pursuers:

"Death to lustration!"

Chest heaving, but now with a gun in his hand, the chauffeur backs away. He wags the gun.

The pursuers hesitate, fearful of bullets. By the time the road is safe enough to cross, the chauffeur has run off in the night.

"What did he say, Vera?"

"Death to lustration."

"Amen to that!"

But Josef is already peering over the river wall. "My case—Milacku, see!"

These aren't tears from Amy's eyes—they're drops of blood.

"Milacku, my case!"

"It's gone, Josef."

Amy is in a suit the quality of whose material and cut and the sheer elegance of its style were made possible only by Auntie's legacy. She fears there's blood on it. What's more, her shoes which had deservedly won compliments from Vera and a lady coming down in the lift, are still scuff-free.

"In the river, Josef," she calls, with as much decisiveness as she can muster. "Forget it—please!"

But Josef refuses to abandon his Pandora. "No—sand-banks. See!" In other circumstances the case would not be discernible from this high point above the river. But the snow-cover on the sandbank makes it as clear as a black beetle on a sheet of paper.

Alan is also at the river wall. Between huge gasps for breath, he adds his support to the old poet. "That case must be rescued at all costs. The Castle must hear the names. That is what Josef wants—what all this is about. The guilty must be brought to book. Long live lustration!"

Amy is sober, resolute. "You want the names, Alan, then fetch them."

Suddenly everyone freezes with terror. Josef has climbed on to the stone parapet. He is gazing up and down the Vltava for a sight of steps to the water's edge.

"Amy!" His appeal goes to her heart. He is in tears. "My case."

"Your bloody case!" she shouts. "Why can't you forget it? Let the past go hang."

"My case, Amy."

In a soft voice, Alan warns, "He's going to jump."

"Okay, okay." Amy is furious. "Come down! If you get down, you silly old sod, I'll go for your case."

Alan cries halt. "Hang on, I want this on film. Jamie, fetch the lights."

"Bugger that," Amy replies. "I'm not going to freeze to death. Come on, Vera."

Eddie makes use of the street light to take a shot of them as they descend the steps. The snow under foot has begun to harden and is slippery with the night frost.

"Torch!" exclaims Alan. "Well done, Sabrina! Thinks of everything."

There is something the tell-tale snow has failed to register. "Oh no!"

Vera says, "Impossible."

162

The sandbank is cut off from where Amy and Vera are standing by several metres of fast-moving water.

The clouds have just opened to permit the moon, and the film crew, a clearer vista of the lonely island on which Josef's case has taken refuge.

All eyes veer towards Amy. "You're the Olympic swimmer, Amy," urges Alan. "Me, I never learnt to swim."

"I am in my best clothes, you prat. Cost me a fortune."

"We'll get it back on expenses. In you go—do it for poetry!"

Amy stands unmoving, her hands on her hips. She stares up at the moon. Is this really happening? Franz Kafka, you ought to be living at this hour.

Of course the Good Soldier Sveyk would have got one of his dogs tipsy and then persuaded it to fetch the case in return for a pound of pork sausages.

Jamie has arrived with lights.

Alan decides provocation is the best way forward. "Don't tell us you're scared of a drop of cold water, Amy Douglas."

"I'll do it," says Vera. "It's probably only waist deep."

Amy glances up. Josef is waving his arms, pointing at Pandora to remind his companions why they are standing about freezing beside the Vltava.

"My case, Amy—my case!"

"The names, Amy—the names!"

Vera is taking off her shoes—high heels, her only pair.

Amy's fury has not abated. "You know what we're doing, Vera? We're being made to carry the can for a bunch of assholes. The old and the proud and the bleeding ambitious."

She bars her friend's way to the water's edge.

Jamie brings light to darkness, transforming the scene into a brilliant tableau.

Sabrina is shaking her head. "It's not right, Alan. She could catch her death in that water."

"Seconds, that's all it'll take. Waist high—maybe less!"

Vera is stepping in to the water. Amy pulls her back. "Me! Only me."

Plaintively from above comes Josef's wail, "Please, Milacku—the case."

She wades in and the river deepens. Great: swimmer in the snow!

The current is strong. Got to laugh, really. How pointless life is sometimes; how ridiculous. Vera would have been swept away, for the few metres are farther than they seemed.

That chauffeur deserved a prize; for shot-putting; another Olympic champion who did not quite make it. I wonder if my necklace will rust.

Amy rises from the waters to a great cheer from the sandbank. The lights are on, the film is rolling. This could be Siberia. She picks up the case.

"Hold it above your head, Amy!"

Soaked and shivering in the back of a taxi summoned by Alan—"Don't worry, the BBC will pay. If not, I'll go halves." Josef has offered Amy his jacket. Very chivalric. They are passing through the gates of the First Courtyard of the Castle. Here, in floodlit stone, an older form of retribution and revenge is being enacted: a semi-naked warrior with a dagger and another with a club deliver death to their enemies.

The presentation ceremony has been delayed. Father Havran is an old hen, clucking with anxiety, now clucking with relief. The sight of Amy dripping all over the ornately tiled floors is a shock. "Whatever happened, my dear?"

"She rescued the List," explains Alan, proudly. "The one Josef is planning to read out."

"The List?"

Vera and Amy are conveyed at speed to a changing room. "What am I going to do?"

Father Havran goes off to search for a change of clothes for Amy. Vera dries her down with a roller towel.

A knock comes at the door. "It is all military gear, I'm afraid," says Father Havran.

"Not that!" cries Vera, pointing at the green Communist uniform.

"I've cut off the insignia."

"It's still a uniform. People will remember they were arrested by men dressed like that, Father."

Father Havran is soothing—and there is no alternative if the ceremony is ever to get started. "Everything will be explained, don't worry. The Minister has arrived, I shall have to go. Please join us in the Vladislavski as soon as Amy is changed."

Vera is remembering she is supposed to be on duty, looking after her Canadians. "What a fiasco!"

"At least you're not freezing to death."

"Oh, Amy, why did you do it?"

"Because the old sod begged me, didn't he?"

"But if there are really names—"

"Well what if there are?"

These trousers must have belonged to a short soldier: they fit almost perfectly. It could be the start of a new fashion.

"Hell, the sleeves!" Not tailored for swimmers' arms.

"Amy?"

"How do I look?"

"Please listen . . . what if I am on that list? What if Jiri's name is there?"

"But they won't be."

"How do you know? The StB, it kept millions of files. In

165

those days you could buy your freedom with names—any names!"

The point goes home. "You're worried most because of your Dad, right? And that is what bugs Jiri."

They are staring into the wall mirror, at themselves, at each other, brown eyes, blue eyes, curly dark, Vltava-soaked blonde. For an instant Vera's face becomes Jiri's; solemn, hurt, quizzical.

Amy reaches back, as if to both brother and sister, draws Vera close to her cheek. "Whatever happens, I shall go on loving you both . . . And I want to say this—never once has Josef said anything to me about names.

"It's everybody else who goes on about them."

Vera's mood has softened. She stares at her friend in the mirror. "How goes the song?—*Two Lovely Black Eyes* . . . You were looking so beautiful." A grin now—shared. "After the ceremony I think we will put you in a pond at Prague Zoo: and call you the Bubble-eye Mermaid of the Vltava!"

Amy turns and gives her friend a hug. She has a better idea:

"No, stick me on top of Jiri's pink tank!"

Chapter Fifteen

The Vladislav Hall, also known as the Hall of Homage, is packed. Given time, Vera would have explained that the Vladislavski was built between 1493 and 1503, that it was 62 metres long, 16 metres wide and 13 metres high and that the design was most noted for its beautiful Late Gothic reticulated vaulting.

On a raised platform at the far end of the room, Josef Sabata sits among dignitaries—ministers of government, a bishop, the chancellor of Charles University, the curator of the Strahov, the British ambassador to Czechoslovakia and numerous directors of theatres—the National Theatre, the Smetana and the Tyl.

The Slovaks are represented here, neatly balancing the Czechs; the Roman Catholics balance the Protestants. Amy's appearance causes glances and frowns. Is this an insult? After years of Communist tyranny, of jackbooted soldiers in green uniforms—who is this girl attempting to turn bad memories into high fashion?

Just put me down as an old English eccentric.

Vera is about to join her twenty Canadians half way down the hall when Amy grabs her by the sleeve. "You're my official translator, remember."

Amy is uneasy and only partly because of her appearance.

Mum always thought green was unlucky. "Never wear it—things go wrong!" Sorry, Mum. It was either this or a monk's robe full of fleas.

Green or no green, something's bound to go wrong: if it can, our Amy, it will—so why fret?

Such is the propriety of the occasion that nothing is said above a whisper about this outrageously dressed young lady, especially as Father Havran, friend of the President, escorts her respectfully to the front of the hall, giving her and her official translator seats next to some of Prague's most distinguished citizens.

They sit. All eyes rest on the girl in the green uniform. Josef's gaze meets her. He winks, explains something to the gentleman next to him. More, he nods towards the ground: Pandora lies at his feet.

Alan and his team have been permitted to film the ceremony alongside two Czech TV crews and one from Austrian television.

"Reconciliation," Alan is saying softly into mike as Eddie's camera pans the audience. "This is the theme of tonight's ceremony, named after the father of the nation, Tomas Masaryk, first president of the Czech Republic, himself a great reconciler.

"Before us, grey hair gleaming in the lights of this ancient hall, where once the monarchs of Bohemia were crowned, is a singular poet, Josef Sabata, returned from exile in a far away country.

"On his entrance here, beneath a magnificent vaulted roof, Josef, once named Kastov for want of his real name, was greeted by a mixture of cheers and tears. The audience rose to its feet and shouted, 'Long live the poet!'

"Yet at this very same moment it is appropriate to ask—what shadows hide behind these joyful faces! What memories of persecution scar their remembrance? Or even what recollections of guilt?

"Are there present those who, for whatever reasons, betrayed a neighbour? Reported on a friend? Gave a name?— when to do so might mean avoiding punishment, receiving a reward—a better job, a better flat?

"Who but heroes would resist?"

The Minister for Culture is greeted with only polite applause. People are unhappy that the President will be absent from the ceremony.

"Flu?" one guest complained. "In the old days nothing but a bullet would have stopped him."

"The Czechs," Jiri had said, "despise all governments."

The Minister for the Interior has also arrived. He gets no applause at all, for he is the Minister for Lustration; the minister of the names. He is quoted as having said of informants during the Communist regime, "They were as bad as the Nazis. We do not wish to work with such people in the new age."

Vera has been looking round at the crowd. "No Jiri."

"Maybe he's mixing some pink paint."

"How did you get on this afternoon?"

"He showed me his etchings."

"Were they good?"

"Okay—but room for improvement."

Vera giggles. "Don't tell *him* that!"

The Minister for Culture delivers a short speech. In it he expresses the President's deep regrets that he is unable to attend the ceremony due to an acute attack of flu. There is a whisper from behind Amy, which Vera translates, "He thinks he might be on Sabata's List!"

Two actors from the National Theatre, a man and a woman, appear on stage. They read a selection of Josef's poems.

169

The speech is too fast for Vera even to begin to translate; so Amy hears sounds and rhythms, the music of the voice— but no meanings.

Vera does at least translate the titles of poems and the time when they were written. About childhood, the loss of everything but the air he breathed; the search, alone, for new beginnings; wanderings in the youthful mind, searching for something to hold, to believe in.

Yet Amy feels the emotion of the audience, its pull, its intake of breath, when the poems speak of the Prague Spring—the briefest moment of liberty, when the crowds took to Wenceslas Square, when suddenly all things seemed possible.

And now, *Swimmers in the Snow*.

Amy shivers. At least here's a poem I know backwards. Who told you, Josef, what happened to us, to Ilona and the rest on our way to the shower rooms, when time stood still at six o'clock?

Who but the dead?

The final poem is the one which will move many in the audience to tears. Somehow it has been kept a secret from Amy, though its title has long been part of her dreams.

Around the hall there is instant recognition, as though the poem were a familiar pop song. Vera translates: "*Child on My Shoulder*—his most famous poem." She knows the poem almost off-by-heart.

> *The child is Spring, the child is hope:*
> *Spring and hope sit on my shoulder.*
> *Alas winter invaded summer,*
> *The tanks brought frost and death,*
> *The Vltava turned to steel.*

> In Wenceslas Square, see the flesh of a lonely youth
> Turn to fire; douse Jan Palach in flowers—
> Martyr to lost liberties. Hear his dying voice,
> "There is petrol enough for all!"
>
> Yet the wind over Petrin is cold,
> Best wait for another Spring. Something might turn up.
> Things could be worse,
> And one day truth will prevail—
> Don't you think?

The poem speaks of the child gone, the shoulder bare, of a lonely tank, unloved and most upset:

> I came to liberate, not enslave
> (At least that's what they told me back in camp).
> You could at least appreciate my position.
>
> Poor tank, so misunderstood.

The poet speaks of the White Mountain in his heart now the child is gone:

> I search the days—no corpse?
> I search the years and death tolls the bell
> On Old Town Clock.
> This prison cell has no terror
> Like your absence, child on my shoulder.

The poet pleads with the absent child, for forgiveness:

> The faceless voice in the shadow
> Said, "Only your silence will buy safe custody,

Only your silence will restore the Spring."

So like Abraham I took the knife to my love:
I raised the blade; yet out of wilderness
No voice came to check the downward blow.

The audience is mouthing the poem's last lines, reciting them along with the actors, almost chanting them:

The child is gone, the shoulder's bare.
Oh child of Spring forgive my silence.
The blade in my hand will one day
Become a pen again, and blood will turn to ink—
Oh believe it!

Something—oh yes, the bells of St Vitus affirm it:
Something will turn up,
Child on my shoulder.

Amy has never experienced anything like this: the power of words to move, to penetrate to the soul. The actors' voices fill the hall, resonate, gather from these ancient walls echoes which seem to have been held in suspense, in restless sleep till now.

The actors finish their reading and for several moments the audience is engulfed in silence.

Eventually the power of silence becomes unbearable: the hall explodes into a thunder of applause, of shouting and cheering.

So that is where it started. She is back at High Lawns, pointing at the picture of the man with the boy on his shoulder. "Is this you, Josef? It certainly looks like you."

"That man is dead."

Now she understands. She stares up at Josef on the platform. Tears will do her black eyes good.

But it is the night Amy is wearing green. One voice brings all things tumbling back to earth: it is the voice of Jiri; clear, though quavering with nerves, and loud.

"Such words are lies!" he shouts. He has stepped from the shadow of his own past.

In the silence which greets his interruption, what he says might be heard all over Prague. "Josef Sabata, you are here to be honoured for the truth of your verses. But there is another truth which has not been spoken tonight."

The Minister is about to summon an attendant; have the intruder ejected, but Josef holds up his hand, as if to say, let him continue.

"Did you not, Josef Sabata, in 1972, or thereabouts, suffer arrest—like so many other brave poets and playwrights and scientists?

"You did. For my father was among those who shared your imprisonment."

Someone is leaning forward on the platform, saying, "Do we have to listen to this?"

"Make your point, young man," says the Minister, "and then sit down."

"I shall, Sir." Jiri is ten or twelve rows back. He faces front and then turns to the rest of the audience. "The man being honoured tonight was once the idol of all those who desired freedom in our country. His poems were read in secret. There were many who were arrested even for copying out and keeping his verses."

The atmosphere is as charged with tension as any that has prevailed in the Vladislavski. "But this man, this frail god, betrayed us."

Vera's arm grips Amy. "Let him finish!"

"Josef Sabata obtained his liberty, ladies and gentlemen, by renouncing his poetry. You will no doubt find the document in the archives of the secret police. But it was public enough at the time. In all the papers, though I know how short memories can be.

"Josef Sabata apologized for his verse, denounced it as he might his closest friend. He consigned his verses to the tyrant's fire. And in return for what—liberty? Freedom to live a lie every waking day.

"Yet now, in this historic chamber, when truth can at last be spoken, this nation honours verses which the poet himself betrayed for thirty pieces of silver!"

Jiri holds up his fists. "Such poetry is tainted for ever!"

Amy understands nothing of this for Jiri is addressing his own people in his own language; but she knows a denunciation when she hears it.

"Stop him, Vera! Please!"

Jiri has not finished. "The people of Prague should rise up, in honoured tradition, and hurl this man's verses out of the window and into oblivion."

Another defenestration of Prague.

"Vera!"

Others are raising voices in defence of Josef; and Vera too decides to act. She shouts, in English, "Enough, Jiri— go home!"

Jiri answers in Czech. "Not quite enough, my sister in shame."

"What's he saying?" begs Amy.

"Nothing good."

"And where has our great national poet been through the years of hardship and tyranny? In safe refuge—pampered in an English nursing home." Against their will, people are listening, compelled. "Until the right moment comes along.

174

The right moment when he can revenge himself upon us; we who stayed behind and suffered.

"We have not assembled here tonight, ladies and gentlemen, to hear Sabata's poems. That is a masquerade. No, let us all admit it. We are here in case he reads out our names— or the names of our loved ones."

Jiri has cast a spell over the audience, touched unhealed wounds. "I would ask, why should we honour him now, when in his hand he carries the infamous case, the one he has preserved with obsessive zeal over the years?"

He presses on to his conclusion. "I would ask—we must all ask—what right has Sabata to expose the names of others who were no worse than him?

"You will be wondering, who is this person who sullies a noble evening? Out of bitterness? Yes; but not for himself. My father suffered as many others did under the old regime. Eight years he spent in jails for no other offence than his independence of mind, his belief in freedom and the good of the community.

"And yet, with the Velvet Revolution, when others received back their jobs, were honoured for their courage, my father was branded with unfounded suspicion. The same will happen to many of you if Josef Sabata is permitted tonight to break his terrible silence."

Momentarily Jiri's voice drops, is almost inaudible. "Such was the shame, my father took his own life." Now he raises his voice, points in accusation at those on the platform. "You betrayed my father. You killed him! All of you!"

This time the attendants are given the signal to remove the speechmaker, but Josef cries out, "No—leave him!" And when Jiri indicates that he has had his say, he is permitted to sit down at the end of a row.

After joy, shock; the onset of numbness. Amy senses the

audience is as stunned as she is. She feels Vera's hand on hers. "It is all over now." There is relief in her voice. "At last!"

Josef is being helped to his feet. This isn't fair. Amy fears for a moment that he will seek refuge in a stupid riddle or stare at the audience as if it had been transformed into an empty television screen.

She glances back at Jiri: I'll deal with you later.

Yet he looks so sad, so shaken by his own words; his own courage to speak. She does not permit him a smile. He does not deserve that. But her gaze does not condemn him to death.

Josef's voice is small, as if emerging from a padded box below the platform; yet the audience drinks in every word.

Vera's head is close to Amy's as she translates.

"Yes," he confesses. "It is no secret. I betrayed my children—my verses. So, too, I remember, did Galileo. Faced with the Inquisition, and being . . . something of a coward like me, he denied the truth to save himself."

Josef unbends his back a little, peers at his audience. "Yet . . . did this make any difference? The earth still spun its course. My poems, that only belonged to me in the making, like my child. They are not my property. They belong to others. To love them, or to burn them."

Amy feels a surge of pride and the tears are flowing again. Her heart is awash with feelings, but strongest among them is pride—that Josef, though accused, is fighting back.

"It is true, my friends, I do not deserve this honour. That I should have disappointed those who loved my poetry, were inspired by it, I am sorry. I have paid my dues, perhaps; in every day and every hour. But none of us must forget that those who hate poets and wish to destroy them . . . they know their business.

"They know our weaknesses. That we fear pain, the loneliness of isolation; we fear rejection—for ever. I am sorry. I did not have the courage of our President, of Vaclav. I understood what I had done.

"But one thing I must say." Here Josef's eyes rest on Amy. His words are for her, for her trust and faith; and fleetingly they take in the half-averted face of Jiri. "Though I betrayed my poetry, turned traitor to it—no man or woman ever suffered from my report.

"When I fled to England it was because I knew myself. The hard men would eventually force me to turn informer on those I loved."

Amy has forgotten her idiotic green uniform, her black eyes, her bruising. She is hearing new poetry from a new man and her heart goes out to old Sir Stubborn of High Lawns.

Josef proceeds, shedding his hesitation with each passing sentence. "I am glad this young man has spoken up. Grateful!" The spark is back in Josef's eyes. "I seek no forgiveness. None from my friends. And none from my enemies. It is too late for that."

Now he stoops, almost loses his balance. Father Havran steadies him. The old man picks up and then holds up Pandora. He dumps it on the table in front of him. The glass over the jug of drinking water rattles sweetly.

"Right, Eddie," warns Alan, "this is it! We need to get in closer."

Josef has removed the key from his neck.

"We'll want a photocopy of those names as soon as he produces them," adds Alan. "Sabrina, are you paying attention?"

Amy is surprised to see tears in Sabrina's eyes.

Josef turns the key in the lock. He takes out an object concealed in a plastic bag. He places it, still wrapped, on the table, with gentle hands—a fond gesture but one which seems to say, ignore this—wait.

He speaks to the audience. He is relaxed now. No more awkwardness; no more stumbling into grumpy silences.

The words flow free as the Vltava, though not so coldly. Josef Sabata is home again. High Lawns is gone for ever.

"In England, when I came out of my long sleep, I wrote a poem, soon to be published, I believe." Here he glances at Father Havran who nods vigorously. "It is called *Pieces of Silver*. Here, my friends, are the pieces."

Josef takes out a silver hairpin, shaped like an oakleaf, holds it up. It flashes in the light.

"Close up, Eddie!" commands Alan.

"Once upon a time, I had sisters. We were separated on our journey to the extermination camps. My elder sister gave me this to remember her by. On her birthday, she was given a crust of bread, a ticket for her clothes—and taken to the gas chamber."

Josef stares around the audience, row by row, face by face. "You want names?"

Many eyes choose to evade the gaze of the poet, seek refuge and solace in the great ceiling of the Vladislavski. They have their own memories, their own tragic losses.

Out of Pandora comes a fob watch on a silver chain. Josef holds it high for all to see. Amy notices that the watch is badly damaged. "This belonged, long ago, to my adoptive father. A Slovak from Brno. It did not save him from the bullet of the Gestapo officer who shot him—for offering shelter to a waif of a boy who appeared, ragged and starving on his doorstep—a Jew and a Czech. He took me in, asked no questions. Loved me as one of his own. A kindly neighbour reported him for harbouring a Jew.

"The watch stopped precisely at six o'clock." Eyes around the hall. "You want names?"

Yes! Amy is answering for herself, in grief and anger: I would give them names. I would shoot them down. But they are dead, the wrongdoers. And I must not hurt their children.

Out of the bag comes a silver bowl, a loving-cup. "This I planned to give to my son. So that he would always remember the day when we Czechs and Slovaks shook our fists at the tanks. Yet our liberties faded over Petrin Hill."

It is left to Alan Francis, impatient with all this talk in a foreign language, to break the spell cast by Josef's recollections. As Josef pauses to pour himself a glass of water, Alan calls out, "Give us the names, Josef! That's what the young gentleman said we're here for."

Josef sips the water, grimaces a little as he notices it has none of the restorative charms of Pivo, and then faces camera as he has become trained to do over the past few hours. "Oh yes, the names. I had almost forgotten them.

"Bear with me for a moment longer." A smile. In English, he says, "You can put the camera on hold at this point, Mr Francis . . ."

"Not likely, chum!"

Josef resorts to his native language. "When the powers that be in Czechoslovakia learnt that Josef Sabata had asked for asylum in Britain, they called me traitor—in every newspaper, on every radio and television station.

"Not one word of my poems would ever again be read by my countrymen and women." A shrug. "So what? I could live with that. But then . . . then came the news of my boy's death. In a road accident. Killed by one of our beloved trams."

So far Josef has caused tears to flow for him; now his own

spill down his cheeks. "The child on my shoulder! That was too much to bear, too much for the mind to hold."

Josef fishes once more into Pandora, brings out a small cotton bag. "Along with the message about my son—sent by an anonymous hand—came this bitter gift."

He unties the cotton bag. He pours coins on to the table. "Thirty Czech crowns from fellow writers in Prague, my friends—thirty pieces of silver!"

The new Josef is never far from a joke. At this moment, he grins. "I plan to spend them on Charles Bridge tomorrow morning!"

At last the tension in the Vladislavski breaks; there is a ripple of laughter. The past is slipping away.

As a sign of this, Josef is holding up Amy Douglas's own gift to him, the silver propelling pencil. "Many years afterwards a miracle happened: the young lady in the green uniform, who this very evening took a dip in the Vltava to rescue my case, stepped into my life."

Josef gazes from the platform at Amy, his expression full of love. "She came out of the blue. Talked to a wreck of a man. A poet who had forgotten himself. She gave him attention and affection—and this pencil, with which I began to write again.

"My guardian angel was, I think, as lost in this world as her Sir Stubborn. But what she possessed was courage—and hope. Amy Douglas?" He addresses her directly. "You made this night possible. You made me whole again . . ." Another grin, "Or at least as much as a Jewish Slovak with bruised ribs can be said to be whole."

More laughter.

Josef does not replace Amy's silver pencil in the case. He clips it proudly to the breast pocket of his new suit. He surveys the faces before him, nods. He has spoken.

The glimmer fades. Amy sees the tiredness sweep over him.

Alan won't be denied his prize. "But what about the names, Mr Sabata?"

The old man remains on his feet. He reaches for the plastic bag, picks it up, holds it protectively to his chest. Then he carries the bag and its contents a pace to the Minister of the Interior—the Minister for Lustration. He permits him a glance inside.

The Minister stands up, his head shaking slowly and in amusement. He returns the object to Josef's case. He addresses Alan and the audience:

"No names!"

"Got to be!" protests Alan, utterly crestfallen. "Everybody knows what's in that case!"

Amy is remembering the Good Soldier Sveyk; the joker with the deadpan face. Old fraud. There were never any names.

"No names!" repeats the Minister for Lustration.

"Well I'll be buggered!" cries Alan. "Half our story's gone down the pan."

Sabrina is smiling. "Don't worry, Alan—you'll think of something."

Amy Douglas finds herself being ushered up on to the platform. Josef has received his medal, but more significant for his future—a state pension.

Cameras flash. The rib-vaulting seems to quiver and melt above her and the audience claps and cheers. She is hugged. Josef holds her hand, raises it—"Milacku! My dear one."

The Minister for Culture has explained Amy's appearance in this strange and provocative garb. He causes a big laugh when he adds, "I assure you she did not purchase it on Charles Bridge, with a Russian tank corps hat thrown in."

"Speech, speech!" It is Vera starting them off, and though

Amy pulls an inane face and shakes her head, the cry continues, "Speech, speech—in English!"

The speech she gives is one word long, and ends in a question mark. It is heard by scarcely any in the audience:

"Jiri?"

This would make the evening perfect—yes, a reconciliation. The words have been spoken. Perhaps they had to be. But the pain—that ought to end now. The past should not hold us in agony.

"Jiri?"

Come forward, Jiri, out of your shadow; out of your grief. Take my hand, take Josef's. Join us in the future. Oh please!

Do that and then this night will really mean something.

She steps down from the platform. She is making the first move: "Jiri?"

The light is poor here. She stares ahead—the chair is empty; the sad starling with ruffled feathers that painted the tank pink, and whose mind and body have drawn Amy to him so powerfully—has flown.

"Jiri?"

Vera is beside her. "Give him time, Amy. It has been all too much. For me as well as him."

Together the friends touch hands, lock hands. Suddenly their attention is diverted towards a figure walking towards them. For a moment Amy thinks it is Jiri, for the young man is the same height.

But the newcomer is limping. He is the man at the airport; the silent watcher on Charles Bridge; the young man who Vera helped stamp his ticket on the tram.

He stops, bows to them in recognition; but his journey carries him onwards to the platform.

Amy in her heart senses the identity of the stranger, but

her head insists on the confirmation of words. She calls after him, "Who are you?"

On the platform, the poet Josef Sabata is staring along the row of celebrities at the young man coming towards him.

"Eddie!" exclaims Alan. "We're back in business. Roll that camera!"

Just in case the young man fails to understand Amy's English, Vera repeats her question in Czech. "Who are you?"

The Vladislavski listens. All listen.

The young man's voice rings out loud enough for everyone to hear. "My name is Sabata." He opens his arms to Josef. "The child on your shoulder!"

Epilogue

"There is a call for you, Amy. Long distance." Sylvia Benson is off for a job interview. "You'd better keep an eye on old Dodds. He's on the scrounge for cigarettes."

Amy is packing. She has a nice room now, second floor, overlooking the swimming pool. A pity they've not bothered to fill the pool this summer—but what would be the point, with High Lawns about to stand empty?

It has taken half an hour to take down her posters and photos and postcards—most of them of Prague; of she and Josef standing under the fabulous clock in Old Town Square; posed with arms linked and raising froth-topped glasses of Pivo in the Black Ox; strolling over Petrin Hill; examining Hunger Wall; wandering the library at the Strahov; placing flowers at the memorial to Jan Palach who made himself a torch of liberty.

Pictures too of Vera, feeding swans in the Waldstein Gardens, walking arm in arm with Josef and his son, Vaclav; pictures of wonder and reconciliation, but always with one face missing—that of Jiri.

"One day," Amy promised herself, "my Prague puzzle will have all its pieces in place." She had left a gap to remind her.

The last picture she takes down is the one she paid to have framed—the newspaper photograph of Josef Sabata in Wenceslas Square, with his son on his shoulder, shaking fists in anger at the Russian tanks and the return to oppression.

As revenge for Josef seeking asylum in Britain, the Czech secret police had reported the death of his son in a road accident. True, he had been knocked down by a negligent tram (a Number 12), and he carries the limp to this day. He was taken to a 'cousin' in Bratislava and told that his father had died among lunatics in a far away country.

In a sense, he had; until someone gave him a silver propelling pencil—and the attention that springs from, and creates, love.

In the hallway Amy meets old Dodds. He has taken up gardening since his chess-playing mate left him to become famous and rich enough to buy himself all the cigarettes he'd ever want to smoke.

Thus it has come as a shock to Mr Dodds to learn that Josef had actually given up smoking. He had made this his excuse when Josef's invitation to visit him in Prague was handed him by Amy.

"No, a man that turns against a good smoke is the man that turns himself against life. I'd like to remember the old sod just as he was. A bloody nuisance. A spy for MI5."

As she passes Mr Dodds, his gardening boots on, spade in hand, sheltering from a light shower, Amy says, "I hope they let you do some gardening in your new home."

Some hope: a hotel on the seafront; and if he misbehaves, what then?

"I don't want to leave, Amy. I can't cope."

These have been sad and bewildering times: things falling apart. High Lawns has been sold to a land developer, its residents have been allocated rooms in guest houses and small hotels.

Can't cope.

Amy knows the answer: it's called freedom. Only there

seems to be more of it for the people up top than we bits and pieces down below.

She has protested to Dr Parrish, who is shortly to take up a post in another part of the country:

"They won't cope, JP!"

"I know, I know, Amy. I am an expert and in my professional judgment the patients won't cope. But who takes any notice of experts these days? The accountants know best. High Lawns was a drain on local resources—"

"High Lawns is a refuge—an asylum!"

"Even for the likes of you and me."

"You didn't fight, Dr Parrish."

"When you reach my age—"

"Josef's much older than you. He'd have fought!"

Was this fair? Is anything fair once you grow up?

In protest at the closure, Amy had stood every evening she was off duty, outside the Council offices, from seven till nine, with a lighted candle in her hand. Clifford had done the same. Mr Dodds had even put in a stint.

She had wondered, if I douse myself in petrol and set myself alight like Jan Palach, would that do any good? She doubted it. The press would accuse her of something or other: had it not reported her appearance in the Vladislavski with the kind of bitterness and unfairness it reserved for anyone who did a good thing?

BRITISH GIRL OFFENDS CZECHS BY WEARING COMMIE UNIFORM.

I probably have Alan to thank for that, as he missed getting his precious names.

Vera: "You should not have told Alan we would celebrate in The Chalice—and then sneak to the Black Ox."

"Served him right!"

Black Ox, Black Ox—where's your laughter and your

poetry now? For Amy, the first celebratory drink after the ceremony in the Vladislavski had been already paid for. The waiter served up the Pivo with a mystery message. Vera translated: "For the blonde lady who swims like a fish."

And the absentee messenger? A young man, as the waiter put it, "with his hair in a pony-tail and all the troubles of the world on his shoulder".

An apology, yet too timid to face her? Well, that apology isn't accepted; and it never will be till you make it yourself. At the very least, Jiri, you could have sent me a postcard of the Pink Tank. I'd have paid for the stamp if you were short.

Nothing.

Amy picks up the phone. "Amy Douglas speaking." It is Vera's second call this week. Josef has been seriously ill. His condition has got worse. "He has been asking for you, Amy."

A sigh. Amy knows—since his release from the prison of himself, since his return to poetry and to old haunts, Josef has treated life as a joyful party which ends at midnight.

Burning the candle at both ends and in the middle—right, old man?

I've got to make up for lost time, Milacku.

But speeches at the Hus Monument? You'll catch flu and worse.

My country needs me!

I've heard that before.

For the Czechs and Slovaks to quarrel, to separate—that would destroy all my hopes.

Then confine your speeches to the Black Ox.

The news that has thrilled Josef the most, that had him phoning Amy after midnight—with the sounds of the Black Ox in the background, is that his son Vaclav has stood successfully for Parliament.

So you're going to marry an MP, Vera.

Who said anything about marriage?

On the phone, Amy says, "Please tell Josef that Milacku is coming. Tomorrow. First flight." A momentary hesitation. "Has anyone else asked after me, Vera?"

"I take it you refer to the bear with the sore head."

"Who else?"

"He is Mister Misery. He avoids me now—I think I remind him of you! At least he has begun to paint once again. Of course he forbids me to see his paintings. But I know one of them is of you, Amy."

"With two black eyes, I imagine, looking like Franz Kafka needing a shave."

Vera confirms that she will be at the airport to meet Amy. "I miss you."

"Oh, one thing—I've got that place at college. They accepted me without the right qualifications, thanks to Mrs Ambler. They were impressed when I said I didn't want to *procrastinate* any longer."

I miss you too, Vera. And Prague; where, as the Good Soldier Sveyk had said: *Every day it goes with a bang there, and should it turn out to be quiet, we'll fix something.*

Oh fix something, Sveyk!

Amy replaces the phone. She stares out over the gardens. The first roses have shed their petals but Sam Peet's green fingers have made High Lawns a glory. "And them buggers," cursed Sam, "the developers—they'll turn it into a tip and me onto the dole!"

High Lawns—about to be sold off; Czechoslovakia—same story, in a way.

Mr Dodds has been watching her. "Is he worse?" A nod. "I said he should never've given up fags. They were keeping him going. You got to have something to look forward to in this life, Amy . . . Now, now, no tears! He'd not want that."

Too late. The poet Josef Sabata died peacefully in the early hours of a June morning in Prague. He had refused to be taken into hospital and no one insisted. He would have his view to the end—out over the Vltava and up towards the Castle and the sparkling pinnacles of St Vitus.

Vera and his son Vaclav have nursed him. They have become close friends and now lovers.

Josef had at least experienced months of happiness and creative fulfilment. He had written many new poems, their themes a far cry from thoughts of dying.

"One of them is dedicated to you, Amy," said Vera; "and it is about you and him. Of course you know what it's called."

Well, not *Swimmers in the Snow*. Not any longer.

Naturally: *Milacku—always!*

They have erected a memorial to the poet—a marble urn on a table of stone. His countrymen are to say their farewells in style. A quartet of string players, in smart blue jackets, is seated in a circle in front of the mourners—a hundred of them—playing a tune that is not altogether sad; indeed it has moments that resemble Josef's riddles.

The President of the Republic has shaken off his flu and his present problems of state. He reads a proud obituary. Father Havran, bushy eyebrowed and eagle-nosed, would like to be reading a prayer. But Josef had ordered—"No prayers, only poems. Or tell a joke!"

Vaclav reads from the latest collection of his father's works.

Amy's head swims with memories. She will not cry. Josef would be insulted. "Remember me as a boring old fart," he'd said, "who liked a pint of Pivo and loved to recite a riddle. That's all it's about, riddles. All a man or woman can do is

189

make the riddles ring, and make your audience laugh."

"It's more than that," she had said, "and you know it."

He had put a finger to his nose; and said nothing more.

The memorial is strewn with bouquets of flowers and wreaths. At the foot of it, on a tiny ledge, is Josef's precious case: Proud Pandora. The speeches are over, the ceremony almost done, though the music of Smetana continues through the warming air.

Vaclav and Vera have held hands. Amy is happy for them. Vaclav limps towards the memorial for the last time. He unfastens the case. He takes out—the names? The secret of life and love and the meaning of existence?—no; but the plastic bag, the contents of Josef had not revealed to the audience in the Vladislavski.

He removes from the bag a Basque cap, faded blue, stained, the peak broken. It is the cap Josef wore the day he jumped from the truck taking his sisters to the death camps; it is the cap worn by the boy on the shoulder of the man in Amy's photograph.

Amy can no longer hold back her tears. Vaclav has turned, approaches her with a gentle smile—a smile she has known so very well till now.

"For you, Amy. He wished you to have it."

"But it's yours."

"My head is too big. Please take it."

She accepts, takes the hat in her hand. And she hears a voice, just beyond the range of all those present:

"Put it on, Milacku—there, a perfect match for your green uniform. You remind me of Sveyk!"

Prague is full of dreams, full of dreamers.

Amy wears the cap. It is right. Pandora is hers also, and its contents, except for the loving-cup which Vaclav will keep, and the brooch which will be presented to the little museum containing the art and the poems and the handmade magazines of the children of Terezin.

It will lie alongside the polar bear with black eyes.

The mourners are disbanding. The President has shaken Amy's hand, kissed her on both cheeks, gone back to the Castle. When Josef had heard that President Vaclav Havel, his old friend from prison days, now used a scooter to speed along the vast corridors of the Hradcany, he had laughed. "He's just a kid, like the rest of us poets. Thank God!"

He had added, "He'll not last. Nothing like that does. At least he'll be able to put aside his speeches and take up his pen again."

Amy waits alone beside the urn of grey-blue marble. Vaclav and Vera allow her silence and distance. "Josef, I've a message from Mr Dodds. He says the fags forgive you for deserting them . . ."

Then tell him I forgive him for cheating at cards!

The musicians are packing up. Their music still hangs in the air, stirred by the scent of flowers. Vera and Vaclav wait for her by the gate. Amy hears footsteps across the gravel: a late mourner, carrying a bunch of flowers the colours of the Czech flag—blue iris, white lilies and scarlet carnations: for sure, a day's pay. Jiri places his flowers at the foot of the monument. He straightens up, looks across at Amy, sheepishly. "How are the black eyes?"

Amy nods. Why feel so confused all of a sudden? "Okay. The better for seeing you."

"Yes?"

She fishes in Josef's case. She holds out the silver propelling pencil. "Josef wanted you to have this, Jiri. All his poems of late were written with it."

Jiri shakes his head, "No, not me."

The fight is in Amy. "Yes you!"

TC   ᴿE
A   ᴀʀE   ᴊOLLEGE
LGNᴰᴼ.. ᴇɪ OPS

Author's Note

On the wall of the Edensor, a small family hotel in Clacton-on-Sea, there is a simple commemorative plaque. It bears a name readers will remember from the dedication page of this book. The plaque records:

IVAN BLATNY FAMOUS CZECHOSLOVAKIAN POET

It then gives the poet's date of birth, in Brno, Moravia, and the period when Ivan was a resident at the hotel until just before his death in 1990. Ivan, a poet of great distinction who spent many years in exile in Britain, is the model for Josef in my story.

Ivan Blatny, like Josef, had his work banned in his own country; like Josef, he was for generations a 'non-person'. Also like Josef, Ivan won due honour in the end. With the Velvet Revolution in Czechoslovakia and the overthrow of Communist rule, the name and the work of Ivan Blatny earned rightful recognition.

That he is remembered at all is due to an English woman whose friendship through the years rescued the poet, and his poetry, from oblivion: Frances Meacham.

What Amy does for Josef in the novel, leading him, through curiosity, determination and eventually love, from a state of mental surrender to a rediscovery of himself and his powers, Frances Meacham did for Ivan Blatny.

It is fitting that when Vaclav Havel spoke at the Mansion House in London during his visit to Britain as President of Czechoslovakia, Frances Meacham was among the distinguished guests. She was presented to Havel on Ivan's behalf. He had been too ill to travel but her report of the event made him very happy.

At the interment of Ivan in a suburb of Clacton, the service was conducted by Father Pazderka, a Jesuit priest who had taken Ivan's poems, collected over the years by Frances Meacham, to their resting place in Prague.

Miss Meacham, a former senior nursing officer, forgives my substituting her in the story with an entirely fictitious character, though Amy and she would, I think, get on well together. Frances Meacham tells me she would be pleased to respond to readers interested in finding out the 'real' story of Ivan Blatny, of how she stored his verses in cardboard boxes in her garage prior to the Velvet Revolution. I would be glad to forward letters to her.

As for Ivan, I think he would see much of himself in Josef. He may well, like Josef, have viewed the splitting of his homeland—on 1st January 1993 —with sadness and some foreboding. Neither, I feel, would be entirely pessimistic if there were those to follow them like Jiri, Vera and Amy.

The Czechs and the Slovaks have begun to go their separate ways. Fortunately no frontiers can keep out the song of the poet.